# CASCADE MOUNTAINS MANHUNT

## JANICE KAY JOHNSON

**Harlequin**

**INTRIGUE**

# Harlequin® INTRIGUE™

ISBN-13: 978-1-335-69077-7

Cascade Mountains Manhunt

Copyright © 2026 by Janice Kay Johnson

Harlequin Enterprises ULC
22 Adelaide St. West, 41st Floor
Toronto, Ontario M5H 4E3, Canada
www.Harlequin.com

HarperCollins Publishers
Macken House, 39/40 Mayor Street Upper,
Dublin 1, D01 C9W8, Ireland
www.HarperCollins.com

**Printed in Lithuania**

1 2 3 4 5 6 7 8 9 10 LIT 28 27 26 25

**"Bill Hayden says you're determined to join the search and rescue group."**

"Of course I am!" Mara insisted. "I have to be there for Brianna."

"If this really is Terrell's plane, the odds of any of them surviving are near zero," said Cam.

"I know. That doesn't change anything."

"I'm leaning heavily on this group consisting of law enforcement, given the evidence that the plane was forced down."

She didn't even blink. "I understand. I'm packed and ready to go. Has anybody spotted debris?"

"The park service helicopter has been in the air for several hours. They're not finding any damage or debris to help narrow the search."

"What if...well, the plane *didn't* go down?"

"I keep asking myself that, but then where *did* it go?"

Mara had no answer.

He let her know that everyone was gathering at the new resort's airstrip.

"In fact, if you're ready..." he said.

She reached for her pack. "I've been ready since you called this morning."

An author of more than ninety books for children and adults with more than seventy-five for Harlequin, **Janice Kay Johnson** writes about love and family, and pens books of gripping romantic suspense. A *USA TODAY* bestselling author and an eight-time finalist for the Romance Writers of America RITA® Award, she won a RITA® Award in 2008. A former librarian, Janice raised two daughters in a small town north of Seattle, Washington.

### Books by Janice Kay Johnson

### Harlequin Intrigue

*Hide the Child*
*Trusting the Sheriff*
*Within Range*
*Brace for Impact*
*The Hunting Season*
*The Last Resort*
*Cold Case Flashbacks*
*Dead in the Water*
*Mustang Creek Manhunt*
*Crime Scene Connection*
*High Mountain Terror*
*The Sheriff's to Protect*
*Crash Landing*
*Black Widow*
*Wilderness Hostage*
*Storing Secrets*
*Explosive Threat*
*Cascade Mountains Manhunt*

Visit the Author Profile page at Harlequin.com.

# CAST OF CHARACTERS

***Cameron Frasier***—An FBI agent undercover as a county deputy, he has his eye on Mara Dawson's family as he investigates major drug connections. His attraction to Mara can't matter, except that he'll do anything to keep her safe.

***Mara Dawson***—A woman who despises lies, she's made her life about Brianna, her niece. As little as she likes Brianna's mother, she never dreams Diana would endanger her daughter when she, her boyfriend and Bri take off on a perilous, one-way flight.

***Brianna Dawson***—Eleven-year-old Brianna mostly trusts her mom despite their clashes...until she realizes that the plane Mom's boyfriend is piloting is about to be shot down deep in the Cascade Mountains.

***Dennis Terrell***—A pilot who owns his own six-seater, he works for a drug cartel until he has an unexpected opportunity to steal so much money, he'd never have to work again. Will he survive long enough to spend a dollar of it?

***Reggie Davis***—A county deputy who joins the search and rescue group searching for the small plane that has crashed in the Cascade Mountains. Does he clash with Cam Frasier because they're both alpha males—or because he has another goal?

# *Chapter One*

At the sound of a faint rattle from the back of the house, Bri Dawson froze with her hand outstretched for the TV remote. She quit breathing while she listened as hard as she could. At last, she stood and tiptoed to where she could see down the hall and into the kitchen. Of course, there was no one in sight, and the only way to be *sure* was to tiptoe as far as the laundry room. She stifled a moan. Now she couldn't even watch TV, because she wouldn't hear someone breaking in.

She didn't like being home alone at night. She didn't even have to be, because Hailey had asked her to spend the night. Mom had said, "Not a chance. I told you already, we're leaving early in the morning." There'd been an edge to her voice when she added, "And no, don't ask again—it's a surprise."

Aunt Mara would have let her hang out until Mom and Dennis picked her up, too. An exasperated eye roll had been the answer to that suggestion. Mom didn't like Bri's aunt, and although Aunt Mara had never said so, Bri could tell she didn't like Mom, either. Face-to-face, they were always polite, even giving each other fake hugs. But Mom usually let Aunt Mara take Bri camping, or shopping down at the big mall in Bremerton. Tonight, she had her back up, that was all.

Well, so what? Bri still had goose bumps. She made herself creep through the house and even looked behind the shower curtain. Then she squared her shoulders, marched to the front door and grabbed her parka. It was only two blocks to Aunt Mara's house, in this dumb little town where Mom had moved them. She could do that. Hide behind bushes when she saw a car coming. She could even run—fast! Mom would be mad, but who cared?

She slipped out onto the porch and pushed the button to lock the door—because leaving it unlocked would make Mom even madder—then dashed across the lawn toward the shelter of a big maple tree.

Two blocks.

THE NOISE LEVEL in the crowded tavern dropped precipitously, leaving a momentary hush. Even before she turned her head, Mara Dawson knew the cause. Sheriff's Deputy Cameron Frasier had just walked in. He didn't carry a gun unless he had one hidden, and he wasn't even wearing his uniform tonight. But dressing down didn't change a thing. He was just that commanding.

He'd only been in town for ten days—Mara remembered the exact moment she'd set eyes on him—and he wasn't yet well-known, but nobody had challenged him, not even jokingly. The night she'd shared a table with him at the café, she could see flickers of humor in his eyes and his lips twitching, but you had to be looking for it or you'd miss any change from the watchful expression that seemed to be his norm.

Even the local band playing tonight hit an off note upon his arrival, but as Cam strolled across the room toward Mara, the voices gradually resumed until the usual din was only slightly subdued. Men pretended he wasn't here, while women couldn't seem to tear their eyes away from him. No surprise there—the man was at least a couple of inches over six feet, long, lean and muscular, and he moved lightly on his feet. He was handsome, but in a hard, wholly masculine way that did it for her, bigtime. That worried her, since he seemed too good to be true. Still…she couldn't remember the last time she'd been this attracted to a man.

He slid into the other side of her booth, the crinkles beside his pale gray eyes serving as a smile. "Hey."

"Hey to you, too," she said. "I'm glad you're here. I was lucky to be able to grab a booth and didn't want to have to fight someone off to keep it."

Before he could so much as lift his hand, a waitress materialized by their table. He ordered a burger and a beer.

The one other time they'd met up here at the tavern, he took sips from his beer but didn't finish it. Maybe he just wasn't a drinker, but it could be that he was too conscious of his role here, in the rowdy town of Thunder Creek, to lower his guard. She herself was nursing a diet cola, and she wished there was somewhere—anywhere—else in town where you could reasonably meet up for a date.

"I see your sister is here," he remarked.

Mara wasn't surprised he'd noticed; he invariably scanned any room before he entered it, and she had no doubt he cataloged every single person in it, even in a crowd like tonight's.

"Not my sister," she said automatically.

"Sister-in-law."

"Not anymore."

Two months back, Mara had snagged her teaching job in this small, sleepy town for one reason and one reason only: she was determined to be close to Bri, her only remaining family. Fortunately, she'd been able to continue her role with the Cascade Mountain Search & Rescue. Diana had been furious, one of the few times their usual civility had broken down, accusing Mara of trying to steal her daughter.

She wasn't wrong: Mara wanted to grab Bri and run, but so far she hadn't discovered a legal justification to excuse her firm belief that the eleven-year-old girl wasn't safe with her mother and the latest of Diana's string of boyfriends. And just wait until Brianna reached puberty!

Aware of Cam's pale eyes intent on her face, Mara forced a smile. "Guess you can tell we're not crazy about each other."

"There a reason?"

"Rubs me the wrong way, that's all."

His gaze stayed on her, and she could see that he knew there was more to it than that, but he had to turn his head to thank the server. He reached for his beer. "Is Brianna safe with her mother and…what's his name, Dennis?"

"I wouldn't give her the Mother of the Year award, but yes." Probably. She grimaced. "At worst, Diana is neglectful. Bri is probably home alone tonight, for example, even though she isn't technically old enough to be on her own. And her birthday was only a month ago!" She let out a huff. "I haven't gotten any bad vibes from Dennis, and Bri talks to me."

Cam nodded thoughtfully. "You ever gone up in that plane with him?"

Dennis Terrell ran a charter business with his six-seater plane. The runway here had been built only four months ago and was private, part of a new resort being built half a mile out of town. Mara had been taken aback when he moved Diana and Bri to this speck on the map bordering Cascade National Park. Would he really get enough charter business here? And why move before the resort opened? The views were spectacular, but Thunder Creek was a long, winding drive through deep forests far from anything you could call a city.

Before the move, he'd operated out of a much busier airport and was apparently thrilled when he could afford to upgrade from the four-seat plane he'd flown for years.

Responding to Cam's question, she said, "I might consider it, if a forest fire was fifteen minutes from overrunning town."

A quick flash of a grin startled her. "Not crazy about him, either?"

Despite herself, she flicked a glance to the side to see Dennis banging his glass on the table to demand a refill. "He's drunk when he's not flying," she said flatly.

"You sure he isn't still drunk when he goes up?"

"I don't think so, but who knows?" She rolled her shoulders to relieve the instant tension. She didn't like the way Dennis yelled at Bri and Diana—although Diana could take care of herself. Mara's brother had been an alcoholic, too. She'd encouraged him many times to go into treatment, then driven him there and picked him up, only to realize two days later he was drunk again. Diana always seemed irritated when he'd go away for a month, though you'd think she'd let out a sigh of relief. Now Mara asked, "Could you cite him if he was?"

"Once he's off the ground, he's technically not my business. I could sure arrest him during his drive to the airport, though. Or make some calls if I knew where he intended to land."

To distract herself, Mara smiled at a passing couple she liked. They smiled in return, but eyed the new local law enforcement cautiously.

It was funny, because she'd bet almost every citizen in here was mostly law-abiding. She hadn't lived here long enough to say for sure, but her impression was that the resident sheriff's deputy—only one, rotating every six months or so—didn't do much but pull over speeders, lurk outside the tavern when it closed down on weekend nights to make sure no one was driving drunk and respond to a rare complaint of something stolen or a citizen who'd locked himself out of his car.

The sheriff's department hadn't bothered stationing anyone full-time in Thunder Creek—and from what she'd been told, *town* had been a generous description for a two-stoplight cluster of log cabins, a pharmacy, a post office, one expensive grocery store and two gas pumps before the resort started going up. Now Whatcom County had expanded the comforting presence of law enforcement by posting one deputy at a time in a minuscule police station that had a single cell in back, sort of like it would have had in the Old West. Right now, two deputies overlapped, and the one who'd been here for six months was apparently showing the ropes to the new guy.

People were way more relaxed around Deputy Walker than they were with Cam Frasier, and Mara totally understood why. Walker was mild-mannered, growing a little soft around the middle and starting to bald, and he seemed to know everyone in town by now.

It was unfair. Cam was amiable whenever she saw him, making an effort to get to know people, never hinting that he could be a threat.

That part, she didn't believe.

A date. Mara couldn't remember the last one she'd been on. She and Cam had run into each other by chance a couple of times and chatted over a meal, but this time, well…they'd planned it.

The startling part was that he appeared to have zeroed in on her as the most interesting woman in town from the moment he set eyes on her. Her gut feeling was that those accidental meetings probably weren't really all that accidental. Of course, she didn't have a lot of competition in a town this small, where most women were married.

Still, she'd been flattered, especially since she had had an unfamiliar reaction to *him* when they met.

Right now, even as he polished off his fries, he watched as she scanned the room, his expression thoughtful. "You expecting a brawl to break out?" he asked after a minute.

Mara laughed. "No, I've never seen one here. Or anywhere else, come to think of it. Occasionally on TV, when I'm watching NFL." She snatched one of his last fries.

His grin would have made her knees wobble if she'd been standing. "Bars around military bases are more volatile."

"How long were you in the military?" she asked.

Between one blink and the next, his expression shuttered. He didn't seem to like talking about himself or at least not about his service. PTSD, maybe? "Couple of enlistments. You go to college right out of high school?"

Tell him? Why should she? "Oh, I worked my way through school. It just took forever. I love teaching."

"I'm surprised there are enough kids around here to fill even a one-room schoolhouse."

"It's not much bigger than that," she admitted. "Middle school and high school ages get bused to Concrete. I feel lucky to have been hired."

Lucky indeed, assuming she wasn't making a huge mistake. One teacher had gotten married and moved in the late summer, right before the regular school year started.

Midnight came and went. The band started playing ballads, and she and Cam danced. She loved the feel of his muscular body against hers, the strength of the arms holding her, but didn't let herself relax entirely. He intimidated her, but after that thought, she immediately corrected herself. She was enjoying the evening but didn't feel that she knew him one iota better than she had when he'd walked into the tavern. That kept her wary. If he really was interested in her, she'd have thought he might open up a little.

He held her hand as they returned to their booth, twice stepping in the way of someone who would have bumped into her. So she knew *that* much about him: he was instinctively protective.

"Another drink?"

Ignoring his half full glass, she said, "No, but I'll keep you company if you want another one."

He smiled. "Nope, but thank you. Can I walk you home?"

She'd driven so he wouldn't have a chance to see her to her door. In fact, unless he'd looked her up in a law enforcement database, he might not even know where she lived. He'd never asked, and like everyone else in town, Mara picked up her mail from her box at the post office. Oh heck, he'd probably seen her pull in or out of her driveway. "No, I have my car."

Too bad.

He did see her to her car and kissed her lightly once she'd unlocked and opened her door. "Wish the resort's restaurant was open," he murmured.

Mara chuckled. "Me, too, except I keep wondering whether they're going to get enough business to stay open. Maybe we should think about a picnic."

She felt his smile when he kissed her again—a kiss that might have gotten more serious if her phone hadn't rung.

Mumbling an apology, she stepped back to dig it out of her pocket. Diana. Something had to be wrong. She wouldn't call otherwise. Mara answered.

"Bri's missing," her former sister-in-law snapped.

"I'm not home."

"I know that!" Diana sounded mad more than panicky. "Some girl wanted her to spend the night, and I said no, but I called there, and the mother swears Bri isn't there and hasn't called."

Mara felt enough panic for both of them. "There's nowhere else…" Or had Bri made other friends?

"I told her to stay home!" Diana said shrilly.

"I'll go home right away in case she let herself in. If she's not there—" If Bri really was missing, Mara didn't even know how to start looking.

Except Sheriff's Deputy Cam Frasier waited a foot away from her, his gaze keen on her face. He would know.

"I'll call," she said hastily, then pocketed her phone.

"Trouble?"

Trying to sound calmer than she felt, she explained, and he said, "I'll come with you. If we find her right away, I'll just walk home."

"Thank you." She squeezed his hand and jumped into her car, grateful that, of all nights, he was with her tonight.

IN THE DASHBOARD LIGHT, Cam saw the tight grip Mara had on the steering wheel. She was more afraid than he'd have expected from an aunt; surely this Brianna had slipped the leash a few times before. On the other hand, Mara's move to a nowhere town just to stay close to her niece was unusual, too. Was this an especially complicated family? Or did Mara have reason to know the kid's mother wasn't reliable?

He'd ask her more about her brother in particular another time, even though he couldn't think why that would immediately impact Mara or the girl now. Unless Dennis Terrell was a more dangerous man than met the eye. So far, Cam was mostly inclined to think he was a loser, but he'd taught himself not to buy in completely to first impressions.

Right now, he held his silence, even as Mara exceeded the twenty-five-mile-an-hour speed limit for the entire five-block trip.

The porch light of a small clapboard house shone in welcome. Mara parked in the driveway and ran up to the house, gripping her keys in her hand. Cam stayed right behind her.

The moment she got the door open, she cried, "Bri! What are you doing here? Your mother is freaking out."

The slender girl, who looked more like Mara than she did her mother, stayed curled up tightly in an easy chair illuminated by a lamp. Looking sullen, she said, "She doesn't usually care. I don't know why *I* had to stay home when *she* was going out. It's not fair!"

Huh. That had a familiar ring to it. Cam had a sister who was three years younger than him. Back when she was twelve or thirteen, Colleen hadn't thought anything her parents decreed was fair. But conflict with a parent could happen at any time, he guessed.

Mara handed over her phone, then stared down at the girl, whose lower lip was still poking out.

"Oh fine!"

Bri had barely started to call when headlights flashed across the front window and a vehicle pulled in behind Mara's.

Ten minutes later, Diana Dawson—who'd kept her late husband's last name —marched her sulky kid out the front door, which Brianna slammed behind her.

The silence left in their wake seemed to vibrate. Cam felt as if he shouldn't have been there to witness the screaming match, but excusing himself would have been awkward.

Mara didn't move for at least a minute, then tossed her keys and phone on the side table and dropped into the easy chair. She gave him a crooked smile and said, "I'm sorry. That was…um…"

"Not your fault."

"No." Her forehead crinkled. "Actually, it was really strange. Diana must have guessed Bri would have come here. She's done that before. Usually, Diana doesn't even notice until morning. In fact… I doubt she even checks to be sure Bri is in bed when she gets home late." She sounded both thoughtful and genuinely puzzled.

Wouldn't most parents check on their kids after an evening out? Maybe not, if the kid was almost a teenager…

He was losing focus. He couldn't afford to be distracted by the family dynamics just because he was attracted to Mara, but he couldn't seem to help it.

She'd caught his eye from the first time he'd set eyes on her. Brown hair often worn in a braid, freckles sprinkled over her nose and green-brown eyes weren't that unusual. Cam thought the magic was in her smile. Who could resist returning it?

And, yeah, her slender, fit body worked for him, too.

Wishing she'd invited him home with her, even though he'd have had to make an excuse, Cam sat down on the ottoman. He was close enough to reach for her hand, but he didn't. Probably shouldn't even do that much. "Maybe your niece swore she'd stay home like a good girl."

Mara wrinkled her nose. "I kind of doubt it. Usually, she's at least honest. Oh well. She needs to learn that it's not okay to take off just because she feels like it. Especially at night."

He could tell she was forcing her easygoing tone now in the hope of hiding how troubled she was. "Far as I can tell, there's not much crime locally," he said gently. "With the construction workers, we've seen a spike in drunk driving and fights, but no more than you'd expect."

Mara nodded. Her hands were knotted at her waist.

She clearly wasn't in the mood for a kiss, which was just as well. Now tension infused her voice. "What I can't figure out is why Diana and Dennis moved here. Bri excelled in school, Diana had a good job, and as far as I know, Dennis stayed plenty busy. It makes no sense!"

Actually, if Cam's suspicions were on target, the move made a lot of sense. Unfortunately, that wasn't anything he could say to this woman, whom he wanted to kiss but needed to keep some distance from.

# Chapter Two

After her mom whacked her across the butt like she was a three-year-old, Bri ran down the hall, slammed her bedroom door and kicked the duffel bag that lay half packed on the floor. Usually, if she could make other arrangements, Mom would let her stay behind when she and Dennis took off for a weekend. She knew Bri was scared of heights, as well as being in the house alone at night. But ever since Dennis came home yesterday from flying a couple of men from the resort somewhere, he and Mom had talked in intense, loud whispers in corners, shutting up every time Bri appeared.

Until right after dinner, when Mom ordered her to pack and said they were taking off for a vacation first thing in the morning.

"Early," she'd stressed, "so be ready."

If Mom and Dennis could go out for a drink, she thought resentfully, what was the hurry? Why would fifteen minutes or half an hour matter?

It was weird how excited and freaked Mom and Dennis looked, though. Mom sent Bri to school sometimes when she didn't feel good, so it jolted her when Mom said, "It won't matter if you miss a day or two of school."

Yes, it would. It was October. Bri was just getting

comfortable with her teacher and making some tentative friendships. Didn't Mom remember what being Bri's age was like?

If she did, she didn't care.

When Bri went to brush her teeth, she could hear parts of what Mom and Dennis were saying in the kitchen. Once Dennis snapped, "Why would they set me up? Everybody gets careless eventually."

"I don't like it—" Mom must have turned away, because Bri couldn't hear the rest. Bri shivered and tiptoed back to her bedroom. She didn't care about Dennis's business anyway.

Right this minute, she hated being a kid and not being able to say, *No, I'm not going.* How was she supposed to sleep?

When the overhead light burst on, it was still dark outside. She bolted upright. "What…? *What?*"

"I told you we were leaving early." Mom was mad once she realized Bri wasn't entirely packed, and the next thing Bri knew, Dennis was shouting, "Well, leave her!" before her mother erupted.

Family vacation. Wow. Cool.

It got weirder. Even still half asleep, once they reached the airfield, Bri saw that except for some security lights on tall posts and a couple attached to the eaves of the hangar, the resort and runways were dark. Dennis had left his Beechcraft plane parked on one side of the hangar. He dropped Bri and Mom off in front of it, unloaded their luggage and then drove away into the darkness. Bri didn't even hear the sound of a door slamming, only the slap, slap, slap of running feet.

He was out of breath when he returned, a silver-colored duffel slung over his shoulder. Once he unlocked the plane, he tossed their bags in the rear hatch of the cargo area and growled, "Hurry, hurry," when they didn't board fast enough. He had to boost Bri, who had hardly grown the past year at all. She was still trying to decide where to sit when he hefted that strange duffel into the seat behind the pilot's. *Fine.* Bri plunked down in the same row, so all she could see was the back of her mother's head.

Instead of fastening her seat belt, she reached for the zipper on the duffel, and he slapped her hand, hard. "Do not touch!"

"What are you doing?" Mom whisper-yelled from the front passenger seat.

"Nothing! I just wanted to know—"

"Dennis's stuff is none of your business!"

Bri clicked her seat belt closed, then slouched low in her seat.

The engines fired up, and it occurred to her that he hadn't done any kind of preflight check, like he always did before takeoff. Maybe he only did it when he had paying passengers, to make them feel safe.

They started to move. With the wheels still on the tarmac, she felt the plane turn, then accelerate. They were still in the dark! Already scared, she tried to see ahead. Didn't he have headlights? There weren't even any runway lights! What if they ran out of runway or veered off to one side or the other?

But neither happened. Her stomach swirled when the plane lifted off the ground and then tilted upward. They climbed and climbed, then banked into a turn.

Bri gripped her seat belt so hard it hurt. She tasted

blood and realized she was biting her lip. Mom and Dennis were talking too low for her to hear; it was like a hiss, lots of tension in their voices. What was happening, and why did they have to drag *her* along?

A thought crept slowly into her mind: maybe because they didn't plan on coming back. Because they were running away from something.

Did it have to do with that giant duffel on the seat beside her? The one she wasn't supposed to touch?

"Where are we going?" she asked loudly.

"Canada!" her mother called over her shoulder.

*Canada?*

MARA SLEPT RESTLESSLY. The night wasn't any darker than usual, but she couldn't turn her mind off. She kept seeing the rage on Diana's face, way out of proportion to Brianna's offense. Mara didn't like how hard she'd yanked Bri out, either, possibly even leaving bruises. Had she had a fight with Dennis? A kicking-him-out kind of fight? Except she and Bri would probably be the ones who had to leave, given that they'd moved here for his job. Anyway, hadn't Mara caught a glimpse of someone waiting behind the wheel of the car?

Maybe he was mad because Diana couldn't control her kid. That would sure get Diana worked up.

Then Mara saw Cam Frasier's face behind her eyelids. It was the last look he'd given her before he left. He had glanced down to her mouth, and she'd swear he had started to bend forward, but then he'd straightened, studied her for that odd moment. The heat in his eyes was belied by the wryness twisting his lips.

Because he knew that wasn't good timing for a passionate kiss, she told herself, but wasn't entirely convinced. It was more as if…he both liked her and didn't. Or wasn't ready to get involved with someone new. Something like that. Her stomach knotted, even as she decided she was reading way too much into his brief expression.

*Flick.* She saw Bri's last, almost pleading glance over her shoulder.

*Flick.* The way Cam kept his gaze on her tonight at the bar, as if no one else was there.

As THE SKY lightened little by little, Bri saw snow and rock through the window. That had to be Mount Shuksan. They were scary close to it. The sharp peaks and cliffs and ragged ice sheets of glaciers were a lot less welcoming than the snow-cone shapes of Mount Baker and Mount Rainier. They were different because they were volcanoes.

Dennis swore. He wasn't looking ahead but instead twisting to see behind them. Bri leaned forward against the tension of her seatbelt to do the same, spotting another airplane close to the size of this one. His radio crackled.

"How did they know?" he yelled.

Bri's usual fear of flying spiked as she saw the glint of the rising sun off metal. Behind them but gaining, she thought. Closer than another plane was supposed to be.

Dennis's Beechcraft started climbing, steeply enough to push Bri back in her seat.

Mom screamed, "What are you *doing*?"

Bri stole a look ahead. She swore they barely skimmed

the ice on the mountain, the frozen peak frighteningly close as they veered past. Was he trying to kill them?

But Dennis steered in a long curve and then sort of dove down the far side of the mountain. This time, Bri's stomach got left behind as they plummeted. Clenching hold of anything she could reach, she twisted her neck so she could see the other plane. Dennis had opened some distance, but it was following even if this was like stunt flying.

Dennis yelled something about a tracker on his plane.

Why would anyone *want* to follow them? Bri wondered, feeling sick.

They zigged and zagged, reversing far enough to swoop close to Mount Baker before dropping in elevation again until there seemed to be nothing but sharp-cut ridges covered with dark forest. Shouldn't he respond on the radio?

The other plane grew closer and closer until Bri could see the two—no, three—men inside it. She couldn't make out their faces, but she thought she saw an open window. She hadn't even known they *could* be opened. Was that safe?

Suddenly, the Beechcraft lurched like it had hit a bird or something.

Mom was screaming, "Call SOS! Or signal that you'll go back!"

"You knew this was a one-way trip," he snarled.

*What? He couldn't mean—*

Something punched a hole in the window inches from Bri's face and kept going to make a bigger hole in the window on Mom's side of the plane.

Terrified, Bri knew: that had to be gunfire. The metal

body of the Beechcraft bucked again. She screamed and kept screaming as the nose pointed down and the giant trees got bigger and bigger. Finally, the tall tips whacked the plane, then kept beating at it.

They were crashing.

A wing ripped from the body. The metallic sounds were terrible. Bri's last thought was, I don't want to die!


CAM'S RADIO SCREECHED, wrenching him from sleep. He groaned, seeing the gray light filtering around the curtain on his bedroom window. There'd be no going back to sleep now.

He rolled over and stabbed the thing. This had better be important.

"Frasier." His voice was morning-hoarse.

"Dispatch here. This may not have anything to do with you, but we've had a call from a climber ascending Mount Baker. He thinks he saw a small plane crash."

Cam's attention sharpened. "Did he actually see it?"

"No, he says a small plane was right behind another one. Passed really close above him, then kept chasing too close to each other toward Shuksan. First he thought the pilots had to be young guys playing chicken, but he swears one of the planes plunged down beyond Shuksan. Out of sight. The other one climbed again to a reasonable altitude and turned to go back southwest. He never saw the first plane again."

By this time, Cam was sitting up on the side of his bed, bare feet flat on the cold floor. "Can he pinpoint the crash site?"

"No, but he's sure it went down in Cascade National

Park. All he knows is that it disappeared on the east or maybe southeast side of Shuksan."

"No beacon has been activated?"

"If so, no one has picked it up."

Or it was out of range. Cell phone service was spotty at best amid the cluster of impressive mountains. Even radio service wasn't 100 percent reliable.

"Okay. I'll get in touch with the park service. We need to get a helicopter in the air. I'll find out who's the head of the local search and rescue, but I hate to assemble them if there was no crash at all. The Canadians might have had a radar that picked up the plane if it went on that way."

Cam switched off his radio and grabbed his phone. The ranger he reached was no happier than Cam was at the early hour and less happy yet when he heard about the possibility of a small plane crash in the rugged, ancient wilderness of the forest. The park service shared access to a helicopter with Mount Rainier National Park, however, and would get it in the air as soon as possible to try to identify a crash site.

Cam rubbed a tired hand over his face. After twisting and turning all night, making a mess of his covers, he felt a decade older. The plane could have taken off from Bellingham or some private strip to the west. That early in the morning, it was no surprise that it had mostly flown unseen.

But he knew better even though he shouldn't jump to a conclusion simply because it fit into his investigation.

Not many small planes would take off at dawn or earlier. There was nothing saying it had come from the single runway here at Thunder Creek…except he'd been gambling that *something* would happen. This might be that something, and he couldn't help reflecting on the odd behavior of Mara's sister-in-law last night.

*Please, God, if this involves that idiot Dennis Terrell, don't let Bri be with him.*

Cam grabbed his phone and tried the numbers he'd been provided for both Terrell and Diana Dawson. Both went straight to voicemail. He would have called Mara next, but he didn't want to scare her before he had something more solid to tell her.

He threw on his clothes, wished he had time for a cup of coffee and drove a little too fast to the single-runway airfield, passing the artfully rustic bulk of the resort itself, still lacking windows and doors.

No planes were parked outside. The hangar doors were closed. Would anyone be here this early? He strode to the metal building and hammered on the door.

Silence, followed by grumbles and swearing. The door swung open. A middle-aged man who had misbuttoned his shirt glared at him, finally blinked and said, "Deputy?"

They'd met before. This was Dave Simmons. From what Cam had been told, the man was in charge of resort development, working below only Victor Levin, whose brainchild it had been. Although Levin undoubtedly had investors, he must have a whole lot of money in it himself. Cam had yet to meet the man.

"Mr. Simmons? We have a report of a small plane going down to the east of Mount Shuksan. I'm here to make sure that plane didn't take off from this strip."

Simmons snatched up a cup he'd set down out of sight and took a long swallow. Cam was tempted to grab it out of his hand and drain the cup himself.

"I can't imagine," the guy said, "but I haven't been here long. Spilled coffee on myself and took a quick shower, so I could have missed something... Let's go look."

Cam let him trot ahead toward the hangar.

"I didn't notice whether Terrell pulled in or not yesterday," Simmons said. "Do you know him? I don't have him down for a flight today. Usually he lets us know, even if it's a tourist show-and-tell he booked separately from his work for us." He fumbled to produce a key ring and soon unfastened the big padlock. Cam helped slide the door up.

One airplane sat in a space that could hold four of a similar size. Cam had made a point of memorizing the make and color of Dennis Terrell's Beechcraft A36 Bonanza, and this wasn't it. What Cam wanted to do was feel for heat on the nose of the plane that was here, but he had no justification at this point.

"Did you see Terrell's plane late afternoon or evening yesterday?" he asked.

"Sure I did." Simmons turned his head as if he'd missed seeing the plane in his first look. "Maybe he took some friends or his family up. He has free run here, at least until we open and have fly-in customers."

"If he took someone up, his vehicle should be here somewhere."

"Unless he got dropped off."

Possible but unlikely, especially at this time of day.

Leaving the hangar, they circled several outbuildings. Cam spotted some ruts heading into a thick stand of hemlock and followed them while Simmons waited behind. A glint caught Cam's eye. It only took a few more steps for him to recognize the extended-cab pickup he'd seen Terrell drive. Empty.

Cam wanted to run, but he took the time to tell Simmons what he'd found and thank him. "I'd appreciate it if you'd check to see if he left you a note or voicemail." He handed over a business card.

*Then* he ran.

THIS WASN'T A school day, but Mara had fallen into the habit of waking at the same time every day. When her doorbell rang, she was only partially dressed—jeans, slippers and a sweatshirt because she hadn't put on her bra yet. *Please don't let this be Diana having lost her daughter again.* After sleeping as poorly as she had last night, Mara would certainly have heard Bri slip in.

Of all people, Cam Frasier stood on her welcome mat. His uniform was wrinkled, as if he'd picked it up off the floor to throw it on. His hair was rumpled, too, and she'd swear he hadn't shaved this morning.

"Cam?"

"Do you know where Terrell and your sister-in-law and niece are?"

"They're—" She stopped. "Bri said something about a vacation. She didn't want to go. Oh no." She clutched the doorframe. "That's why Diana was so mad last night."

"Terrell's plane is gone, and his truck is hidden in the woods a short distance from the runway."

"But…why would anyone notice?" She had a bad feeling she was being dense. Cam wouldn't be up at the crack of dawn, knocking on her door, without good reason. Even so, her mouth kept moving. "I mean, unless he had a job booked for today."

Regret deepened some lines on Cam's face. "A climber on Mount Baker believes he saw a small plane go down. We've been unable to reach Terrell or your sister-in-law. We're far from sure right now that it was him, but—"

She absorbed what he was telling her. He'd softened his message, but he *knew*, she could tell. He must have been roused out of bed to rush out to the small airfield and make sure no plane had gone missing.

"They have Bri with them," she whispered.

# *Chapter Three*

Cam was fortunate enough to reach the cell phone belonging to the climber who'd reported the potential crash. He sounded a little uncertain, but his description of the bizarre event hadn't changed.

"I mean, it could have been a game or something. It's just…"

Cam waited.

"The plane was heading down too steeply," the climber finally said.

"Do you recall what color either plane was?"

"Uh…" His voice became muffled as he apparently spoke to a fellow climber. "We both think the one in front was white with blue stripes. You know. Neither of us are sure about the other one."

Dennis Terrell's Beechcraft was white trimmed with blue.

The guy gave better coordinates for where his party had been on the mountain. Cam heard crackling on the other end, as if the guy was getting a map out of his pack. "If I were going looking for it, my best guess is somewhere south or east of the Chilliwack River area. I could be off by miles, but—"

"We're getting a helicopter up to look for evidence of

a crash site. Thanks for taking my call. We may eventually hear from other witnesses, but it's equally possible nobody else saw what happened. Any backpackers in the area probably weren't awake yet." By October, hikers and climbers wouldn't be as numerous as they'd been a month ago. "I'd much rather get search and rescue out than have somebody stumble on the wreckage next spring. You did the right thing."

Cam made his next call to his park service contact, who did not sound optimistic. "You know about the big fire out there. The Chilliwack River area and Copper Ridge have been closed for a couple of years. Only positive is that a downed airplane would be easy to spot there." He made a humming sound. "Brush Creek, Whatcom Pass, maybe? Because access is difficult, I'm guessing the closest peaks aren't attracting the usual number of climbers, either."

"The guy climbing Baker was sharp, and he was looking at a topographical map when we spoke."

"Okay. Do we call out search and rescue yet, without being able to narrow the location?"

Cam had been asking himself the same question. "I think I'll make contact with the coordinator and see how many volunteers we can drum up, even if we're still on pause. That can take time. Then there's the question of how we get there."

The park ranger grunted agreement. Searchers on foot would likely have to walk many miles before they even got into the vicinity of where the crash would be. At this point, he hoped the park service helicopter spotter would see *something*. The odds were somewhat improved because of the time of year; at lower elevations, maple and alder trees would be leafless or shedding the few that remained. One glimpse was all it would take. If so, the copter could come back for the first group of search and rescue people and deliver them as close as possible to the site. Alternatively, Cam believed he could commandeer a helicopter or two from the Whidbey Island air force base.

Finally, Cam said, "I'd appreciate it if you'd keep this to yourself for now, but I have reason to believe this plane was deliberately brought down. I'm a federal agent under cover as a Whatcom County deputy to investigate the pilot and his associates. We can't risk taking just anyone to search."

After a small silence, the ranger said, "We had a small plane brought down by a bomb a few years ago. Real ugly. One woman survived by what had to be a miracle. In this case…"

"I heard about that one," Cam said. He'd read about the trial, at which she'd been the principal witness, too, the reason the defendant had done his best to eliminate her before she could step into a courtroom. "If my suspicions are right, the pilot had a woman and an eleven-year-old girl with him."

The ranger really wanted to know more, but Cam hedged. He didn't yet have any evidence that the resort was being built specifically to provide easy access to the Canadian border and transportation of illegal drugs, possibly human trafficking or simply a way for members of whatever kind of syndicate funding the place to meet without making standard border crossings. He would've appreciated having considerably more information before responding to what might well be the violent deaths of Dennis, Diana…and the young girl Mara loved so much.

Bri lay very, very still. Somehow she knew it would hurt to move, even to lift her hand to her face. She drifted for a while, but a tiny corner of her brain kept working. Where was she? Why did she feel so awful? She vaguely remembered going to bed, mad because of Mom's yelling and because she didn't understand what Dennis said. Could she have gotten sick during the night?

She really needed to open her eyes. A throbbing in her head told her that wouldn't feel good, either, but she had to know what was wrong. One at a time, she pried her eyes open. Not her bedroom, she could tell that much. Without turning her head to look side to side, all she saw was green. Rich, luminous shades of green. Were those sunbeams slanting between the slats of her blinds? No, not blinds.

This wasn't any kind of room. Those were twisted bare branches, but mostly she saw the giant evergreen trees above her, the sun's rays barely touching the green beneath her, which felt…squishy to her touch. Damp, too.

She kept staring up, seeing filmy cloth draping over tree branches, shivering just a tiny bit occasionally. She knew that was lichen. Even Thunder Creek lay in what was called a temperate rain forest. Her teacher, Mrs. Bailey, had explained that a rain forest was called that because— duh—so much rain fell. Most rain forests were tropical, like in South America.

So…she was lying on what the textures and colors told her was moss. Thick, forming a deep pad that felt like lying on a super expensive mattress, like the ones in the store where she and Mom had pretended they were serious shoppers when there was no way they could afford anything there.

*Mom.* Where was Mom?

Memories flickered through Bri's head. *Dennis.* Shouldn't he be here, too? Wherever here was?

And then, as if a dam had broken, she remembered Dennis slapping her hand, then piloting his plane in complete darkness. Taking off. Mom saying they were going to Canada, and Bri realizing how weird this was.

Not a vacation.

Inevitably, the awful part scrolled behind her closed eyelids. Another small plane following them. Dennis swerving frantically, a wing practically skimming crumpled ice on…one of the mountains.

He'd yelled something about how there must be a tracker on his plane.

The last, awful thing Bri remembered Dennis saying was, *You knew this was a one-way trip.* He hadn't meant that to say, *We'll all die.* Had he?

Bri's stomach heaved, and she had to roll to the side to puke. It hurt, but her stomach didn't care. She puked until nothing was left, then kept on as if she wanted to expel even the pain.

A bullet had whizzed right by her. At least one more had made the plane spin, like on a scary ride at the fair. After that, she didn't remember, except they fell from the sky.

So why was she all by herself, with no airplane, no Dennis, no Mom?

She had to find out, even if she was desperately afraid to.

CAM HADN'T COME BACK, which didn't surprise Mara. Surely he'd have called to let her know if he'd located Bri and Diana safe and sound. Since he hadn't, he'd be tied up for hours consulting with someone at the park service, maybe even Canadian border patrol, and probably rounding up search and rescue volunteers.

She was actually surprised she hadn't heard from Bill Hayden, who served as coordinator for the loose group of volunteers who got called in for search and rescue for not just the national park but also the several vast wilderness areas surrounding the park. Bill's back had deteriorated to a point where he couldn't join rescues himself, but he knew everything, including who lived where. He would focus his calls on those best placed geographically.

If she didn't hear from him soon, she'd call him. If she had to go all by herself, she would—once she could wring more information from Deputy Frasier, who was close-mouthed enough to try to keep her out of this.

Well, she'd make sure she was ready to go the instant she got the call. In a pinch, she could grab her pack and go, but given the chance she always went through it to be sure there wasn't something extra she should add, maybe replenish medical supplies or food. Only a few weeks ago, she and four other volunteers had brought an injured climber down from Mount Triumph, eventually loading him into a helicopter to be carried to the hospital. The trouble was, right now she didn't know whether the plane that might or might not be Dennis's had come down on ice and rock or slammed into a heavily forested ridge.

Her heart felt as if it were knotted in a ball, like a fist with knuckles turned white. Her mind tried to play through various scenarios, but she couldn't let it. Not when Bri was in that airplane.

Her phone rang. She snatched it up before it could ring a second time.

"Mara?"

She knew the voice. Bill, as she'd expected.

"It's me. I…already know about the plane crash. Has the site been located?"

"Unfortunately not. Authorities still aren't certain a plane really went down, but it's sounding likely. It never arrived in Canadian airspace, and air traffic control at surrounding airports are sure it didn't appear on their radar, either. We're putting together a group that can be ready to head out at a moment's notice. Of course I thought of you right away, but I understand it's possible the plane was your brother-in-law's and your niece was on it. That can't be something you should see. I wanted to give you the option, but I'd recommend you sit this one out."

"I'm going. Wouldn't you, if Olivia were missing?" Bill's phone was full of photos of three-year-old Olivia. He whipped it out at the slightest excuse to show off his cute grandkid.

Voice heavy, he said, "Yeah. Okay. I'll let the deputy stationed up your way know."

"Is Deputy Frasier making the decisions?"

"So far, it's his show. The only other law enforcement officer that close is Deputy Walker, and he's not up for a ten-mile hike, never mind ascending three thousand feet or more."

She had her doubts that Walker was up for a three-mile hike on flat ground. It was just as well Cam had been assigned here, but she'd had the impression he was newly hired by the county. You'd think they'd want a situation like this to be run by an experienced deputy already part of the SAR group. But maybe she was wrong;

Cam hadn't actually said that he was new on the job. He'd never mentioned the police academy or where he'd been stationed. Given his disinterest in expanding on his history, all she really knew about him was that he was former army.

Gee, no wonder she still felt as if the man was a stranger, no matter the glint in his eyes when he looked at her.

"Who else have you lined up?" she asked.

"The only solid yeses are both park rangers you know. I can't guarantee them, because Deputy Frasier wants to okay everyone in the group."

"That takes some nerve."

"He's concerned because the one report suggests this was no accident."

She'd known that but not allowed herself to take the logical next steps. Why would Dennis's plane have been forced down? Why had he and Diana seemed so wound up? He wouldn't have stolen something, would he? Mara wanted to dismiss that possibility immediately but couldn't. Dennis was sleazy, and that was putting it kindly.

Would Diana go along with something like that? Mara greatly feared she would. But would Diana risk Bri?

Mara would have said no, that Diana loved her daughter, but she wasn't the greatest caretaker, either. So... maybe. Either that, or she'd let herself be blithely unaware of any potential danger.

Still...what were the odds searchers would find themselves under fire or whatever else Cam was thinking? Maybe he was flashing back to his military service. If so, he might not be the best person to be in charge.

Except she didn't quite believe that, not given his effortless air of command and competency. He had to have been an officer.

*Call. Please call, Cam.*


BRI EVENTUALLY REALIZED one reason she was having such a hard time sitting up was that her head was way lower than her feet, and she didn't exactly have the kind of rock hard abs she'd seen on a shirtless Chris Hemsworth in *People Magazine*. He might be an old guy, but he obviously worked out. None of the boys in Thunder Creek looked like that when they played soccer or flag football or whatever when the weather was hot this summer.

Why was she thinking about something like that?

Because she didn't want to try again. Wriggle sideways, she decided. Sort of…inch around, until her feet were downhill from her head. Maybe her head wouldn't hurt as bad then, too.

She managed, but it took time. Panic felt like a reaction she'd once had to a shot a doctor had given her, only it spread through her whole body.

Also…did she *want* to see? If either of them were okay, wouldn't Mom or Dennis be looking for her? Or at least have called out?

Her teeth chattered as she struggled to sit up. In fact, she thought all of her was trembling. And, ick, there was her own puke. Only somehow she didn't care. Moving carefully, she turned her head. All she saw were the enormous trunks of trees, feathery limbs reaching for the ground, moss everywhere it could cling, low junglelike growth in some places. And a glint of water… a creek that probably ran way higher in the spring and early summer when snow melted up above. Right now, water shimmered as it wound between boulders, some of which were half covered with *more* moss.

Oh—there was a sort of dam made up of sticks. This was a beaver pond. Aunt Mara had pointed them out before. In fact, was that dark ripple an actual beaver?

What she didn't see was an airplane. What if that bullet through the glass had made the window implode and she'd been sucked out because of pressure?

Yeah, but that happened because of altitude, Bri thought. Plus, if she'd gotten sucked out and fallen through those giant trees to the ground, she probably wouldn't be alive to be sitting here wondering this stuff. Plus times two, she'd worn a seat belt. Unless somehow she'd released it when she grabbed the belt in terror. Where was the seat?

Swallowing, she made herself rotate on her butt, looking one way, then the other, and finally behind herself, where she caught the first glimpse of mangled metal. A single seat sat in the midst of it, still attached to the metal. That had to be *her* seat, didn't it?

But then, where was the rest of the airplane? Where was Mom?

THE CALL CAM had been praying for came in before his tension started developing hairline cracks. It was routed through the park service.

"Uh… I think I saw a plane crash," said a woman, voice high and tremulous. "I'm not positive, because there wasn't a fireball or anything like that, but…"

"First, thank you for calling," he said in the voice he knew best calmed people. "Tell me where you are."

"Oh!" She sounded startled. "We were on Little Beaver Trail, almost to Ross Lake."

"Were?"

"I didn't have phone service, so my friend and I jogged until I could call."

"What exactly did you see?"

Her story wasn't dissimilar to the climber's. She'd seen what appeared to be one plane chasing another, until the one in the lead kind of skewed sideways—her words—and dropped fast out of sight. Which probably hadn't taken long, given the heavy tree cover and steep ridges climbing toward a formidable mountain range to the east.

Not an accident, he told himself grimly.

"I didn't hear anything, but I think I'd have seen it if it was able to climb high enough to go on," she concluded. "And the other plane half circled and went back the way it came."

She and her friend thought that second plane was white with some red on it, but weren't positive. Cam's jaw tightened as he pictured the six-seater parked in the hanger at the new Thunder Creek Resort. Unfortunately, a witness account from someone who "thought" the plane was accented with red wouldn't be enough for a warrant.

The hiker's best guess put the crash this side of the Picket Range, maybe Picket Creek or Mineral Creek. Country that was truly wild, not accessible by maintained trails. It had been made even more inaccessible because of the fire that closed the Chilliwack Ridge trail loop.

He was already calculating. On the map, what he was looking at were extremely steep drops into river valleys and climbs just as daunting up the next ridge. They'd be very, very lucky if local wildlife had left even a rough trail to follow.

Bri snatched at a low tree branch to steady herself. Her legs had wobbled from the moment she managed to get to her feet. She had no idea if she was going the right direction to find more pieces of the plane, but she had to search until she found it. Mom might be hurt but alive. Maybe *she* was searching frantically for her right this minute.

Bri tried calling out a few times, "Mom! Dennis!" but if anything, the surrounding woods grew quieter. Once, she fell down when a blue jay screeched and took off right in front of her. Getting back up was even harder that time.

Weirdly, the first part of the plane she spotted was another seat. It had to be the one next to hers, because she caught a glint of silver deep in some ferns. That stupid bag, the one she had a feeling was the cause of all this.

She ignored it and tottered on. "Mom? Mom?" Her voice trailed off. "Where *are* you?"

Scared, feeling more alone than she'd ever been, Bri knew that if her mother could answer, she would.

"Please, please, please," she whispered and scrambled over tumbled rocks.

# *Chapter Four*

The knock on Mara's door came an eternity later. Tall and stern, Cam Frasier—no, *Deputy* Frasier, she reminded herself, stranger that he remained despite their dates—stepped in after she held open her door.

"Bill Hayden says you're determined to join the search and rescue group."

"Of course I am! I have to be there for Brianna."

Deep lines formed on his forehead. "If this really is Terrell's plane, the odds of any of them surviving are near zero."

Her stomach flipped. "I know. That doesn't change anything."

"I'm leaning heavily on this group consisting of law enforcement, given the evidence that the plane was forced down."

She didn't even blink. "I understand."

After a moment, he sighed. "We're also lucky enough to have a serious climber named, uh, Joe Walden and a doctor."

"Daniel Cardoza? Oh, that's great!"

"Is he in shape for traversing rough country?"

She actually found a smile. "He's a triathlete. Could probably run circles around the rest of us. I don't know if Bill said, but Daniel works as an ER doc and has been doing search and rescue forever."

"Ah. No wonder Bill pushed him at me." He sighed again and frowned down at her. "You're sure?"

"I'm packed and ready to go." She bit her lip. "Has anybody spotted debris?"

"The park service helicopter has been in the air for several hours. They're not finding any damage or debris to help narrow the search."

"What if…well, the plane *didn't* go down?"

Cam shook his head. "I keep asking myself that, but then where did it go?"

Mara had no answer.

He let her know that everyone was gathering at the new resort's airstrip. He had a peculiar expression when he said that, as if… Well, he was smart enough to wonder if Dennis had gotten himself in trouble, and if so, the resort was his primary employer. Yet the search party would be an expected response. She only wondered if he knew more than he'd told her.

"In fact, if you're ready…" he said.

She reached for her pack. "I've been ready since you called this morning."

Cam grimaced, took the pack from her and carried it out to his truck.

Bri grew shakier and shakier, her vision fogging as if she were underwater. The sun was climbing high in the sky, which told her hours had passed. She must have lost consciousness, although she had no idea how long she'd been out for. Weirdly, she felt cold despite it being a sunny fall day.

She found more bits and pieces of the plane, which kept her going. Otherwise, she might have turned around and tried a different direction. Her arms and face stung from the low bare branches she grabbed to stabilize herself. The ferns she recognized, but the roots and trunks of everything else were just obstacles that kept tripping her.

She was more or less following the creek, for a lot of reasons. She could start going in circles if she didn't have that much guidance, at least. And it made sense that Dennis might have tried to steer for the slightly more open creek running between steep ridges, right?

A large blob of white caught her eye. It appeared to be wedged between the giant scarred trunks of firs or hemlocks.

Oh God. "Mom?" she whispered.

Nothing stirred. A tiny bird fled from a branch almost in arm's reach.

Bri wanted to tiptoe, but the ground was way too steep, rocky and deeply shadowed by a very old forest. She had to crawl.

This could be the back of the plane. She wouldn't mind that too much, because she desperately wanted something warm to put on, and that was where all their bags had gone. Except, of course, the strange one she wasn't allowed to touch.

A propeller blade had ended up sliced into the trunk of one of those trees. Bri felt sick, seeing that, and how crumpled the wreckage was, spilling airplane innards, especially wires and wads of something white. Insulation? *Her* seat could have been reinstalled in a plane, no problem. Nothing about this was salvageable.

"Please," she whimpered.

Could she bear—? How could she *not* look?

Her feet kept sliding. Her palms were raw, seeping blood as she tried to pull herself upward. It wasn't that far, but seemed to take forever.

Bri saw Dennis first, his lower body crushed by the plane, and his head…

She went to her knees and tried to puke again, except nothing came out. Had he been *shot* in the head? Flies buzzed, and she couldn't make herself look more closely, but remembered the first bullet that had passed inches from her and through the right hand window.

Bri sobbed, tears and snot running down her face. She used the hem of her shirt to wipe her face so she could see. Because she *had* to.

That meant backing down a short ways, then scrambling up beyond the other forest giant. Unless Mommy had been thrown clear… But Bri knew better.

What she saw wasn't Mommy. Well, the hair color was right, but otherwise… The horde of flies and pieces left from the plane made it worse in one way and better in another. All she could do was stare.

After a minute she sagged to her butt, pulled up her knees and buried her face in them. The first sob tore through her, and they kept coming.

"You ever ridden in a helicopter?"

Mara looked at Cam like he was nuts, probably because the search and rescue—known among themselves as SAR—volunteers of necessity often had to be flown into the back country. If he hadn't done SAR locally, where had he gained experience?

All she said was, "Yes."

Which didn't mean she liked them. She didn't love flying at all, but the racket and the shaking and the vibrations she could feel in her bones rated helicopters at the bottom of her acceptable forms of transportation list.

The two sheriff's deputies arrived together in a marked car. Mara knew one of them, Lori Holmes, who hugged her and murmured in her ear, "I hope to God Brianna wasn't on this plane."

She returned the hug, blinking back tears. She couldn't let Cam see them, or he'd decide she was too emotional to go on this expedition.

When Lori stepped back, she said, "Do you know Reggie Davis?"

"No. Are you new to the area, or have we just happened not to be in the same SAR group?" Mara asked.

"I'm new to the department. Moved up from Oregon." His forehead creased. "I hear there's a chance someone you know was on this airplane?"

"I'm…hoping that's not the case. It's good of you to join us."

Cam stepped forward to introduce himself with a stiff handshake.

Mara was surprised not to have heard any chatter about this Davis guy; usually by the time a new volunteer was welcomed into the group, he'd been vetted by current members who'd hiked or climbed or skied with him. There had to be a level of trust.

Of course, in this instance, Frasier's insistence on only gun-carrying volunteers might explain the inclusion. It was always tricky for the cops, who couldn't slither out of a working day as easily as other volunteers.

Even though it was Saturday, Mara had already left

a message at the school district offices explaining the possibility of her being absent on Monday and Tuesday.

Ten minutes later, Joe appeared in his shiny, new extended cab pickup truck. In his mid-fifties, Joe hopped out as if he were two decades younger, locked his vehicle and grabbed a massive pack festooned with climbing rope from the bed of his truck. He lived in Concrete and owned several businesses. Mara had found him to be reserved, not as openly friendly as some of the others but she'd seen nothing but determination and compassion in him.

Cam shook hands with him, too, and also with Dr. Cardoza when he showed up. He was taller than most distance runners but still wiry.

"Are we it?" Joe asked.

Cam replied, "No, two park service employees will be on the helicopter. We may need more folks, but I want to be cautious initially. You all know why."

"Given how much territory we have to cover, a hundred volunteers wouldn't be too many," Reggie pointed out.

"No," Cam agreed. "Problem is getting them into our target area. Hiking, climbing and bushwhacking in could take days."

Dr. Cardoza said, "I wish we had a closer witness. Unless we find that plane right away, I won't be much help."

Mara winced. Well, at least he was pretending he thought they might find injured as well as dead if only they hustled fast enough.

Cam's upper arm bumped her shoulder, and although he wasn't looking at her, it had to be deliberate. "I was grateful for the second caller. She was able to see more."

The doctor shrugged acceptance.

Cam said, "You're all aware of the possible danger

during this search. There's a reason I wanted as many of you to be armed as possible–and that the park service agreed to us carrying weapons despite the usual ban."

People glanced at each other, but gazes were primarily steady. Yes, Mara guessed they all felt the tension, but SAR members accepted significant danger during any rescue, given how rugged these mountains were.

To Mara, the wait for the helicopter felt interminable. She was grateful when Cam glanced down at her. "You moved here only recently. How is it you know everyone?"

"I used to live right outside Bellingham, and in a sprawling way we're all part of the same SAR team. I've done rescues on Baker, Shuksan—never Glacier for some reason—and lots of surrounding national and state forests as well as the park."

"Ah." That was it. From then on, she and Cam stood in silence while the others spoke quietly to each other. His expression didn't change, but she'd swear he radiated impatience and frustration. Or maybe *she* was the only one who hated every second of delay.

All she could think was, *We're coming, Bri. I swear we are.*

SHE REALLY WAS alone and had no idea what to do next. Bri felt like a coward, but she couldn't make herself look at her mother or Dennis again. She didn't have to. All she had to do was close her eyes to see them as if for the first time.

Finally, she skidded on her butt down the steep side-hill until the ground was slightly flatter and she could hear the creek again.

She did know what to do, she realized, as if Aunt Mara

had spoken firmly in her ear. She had to find the rear of the plane in hopes the luggage hadn't been strewn halfway to Canada. Someone would be coming; she needed to have faith. If nobody else came, Aunt Mara would. Bri really believed that. And she'd expect Bri to have used common sense. That was what she always said. She'd showed Bri some of the ways to do that when they hiked or backpacked together.

Warm clothes, the boots she'd stuffed into her duffel at the last minute and food. She hoped Dennis had carried emergency supplies, including something to eat.

Looking upstream, Bri didn't see any sign of more scarring or flashes of white metal. That didn't mean the back of the plane hadn't been flung ahead. The plane must have flipped when they came down, but if the nose was here, and her seat was behind her, it stood to reason the luggage compartment was even farther back. If she didn't find it that way…she'd just have to keep searching, even if that meant scrambling up the ridges that climbed so steeply on each side of the creek. She couldn't bear to climb over Mom and Dennis's body to look for anything useful. No. Just no.

As she trudged, slithered and, in spots, crawled back the way she'd come, Bri remembered Dennis yelling about how there had to be a tracker on his plane. She had no idea what one would look like, and with the debris spread out over so much ground, finding it would be next to impossible. If "they" had planted a tracker on Dennis's plane, "they" would be the ones coming, and she didn't want to meet them. Which meant she had to get a good distance away before anyone locked onto the tracker.

Only…what if the tracker hadn't been attached to

the plane? What if it had been in the mysterious bag? That made more sense, didn't it, especially if something valuable was in that bag. For all she was feeling now—exhaustion, pain and grief—Bri felt a new emotion stir: rage.

"They" had killed Mom, and Bri wasn't going to let them have back whatever made them do it. She'd hide the bag someplace where she could find it again but they couldn't.

But first she'd search to be sure there wasn't anything in the bag that could possibly be a tracker. And she'd do that before she continued the search for the cargo area. Being mad helped her push back every other awful thing she felt.

By the time she fell to her knees next to the silver bag, she wasn't sure she'd be able to get up again, but she had to. She'd just rest while she was finding out what Dennis had likely stolen.

The stiff, heavy metallic fabric really was strange; she'd never seen a duffel like this before. But then she remembered… Mom kept what she called important papers in a big envelope that was this color and texture. Because it was supposed to be fireproof, Bri realized. Had Mom brought those important papers? Or left them behind?

Squatting there, she wondered for the first time about their phones. Those could be traced somehow by GPS, so maybe they'd left them behind, too. If not, they'd have been in pockets or Mom's purse. No way she'd go back and… She shuddered. No.

Besides, Aunt Mara said phones hardly ever worked in the mountains.

Her hand shook as she reached for the zipper. It didn't slide smoothly, not at first, but finally she tugged it all the way down. Then she stared, almost as shocked as she'd been at the sight of Dennis and her mother.

The bag was filled with money. Neat piles bundled and fastened with rubber bands. The ones on top she saw at first were hundred dollar bills, but there—that one was a *thousand* dollar bill. Bri didn't even know money came in that denomination.

She lifted a few bundles out at random, seeing only identical ones beneath them. Had Dennis stolen it? Normal people used banks for transferring money like this, but Dennis…there'd always been something sleazy about him. Something that had made her aunt uncomfortable.

She couldn't even imagine how much money she was looking at, but she understood why somebody would be furious if all this had been stolen.

Did Mom know what he'd done?

A lump formed in Bri's throat. No, she should ask whether Mom *had* known. Mom was dead.

Of course she had. There must be enough in here that she and Dennis thought they could buy a fancy house and really nice things and maybe not have to work for a long time, if ever. The catch was, they had to get away, and they'd failed.

*You knew this was a one-way trip.* Wasn't that what he'd yelled at Mom?

Bri shivered and realized the sun wasn't as high in the sky anymore. *Quit looking at the money and find out what else is in here.*

There was a note, hand-scrawled on a Post-it and stuck in the top of one of the bundles. It said, *As Promised.* Bri was careful not to touch it, in case it had fingerprints or DNA or something on it. That was what detectives on TV were always looking for.

She did grope around the bundles of money, which took up most of the space. If the tracker was like those nickel-size, flat batteries, it could be stuck between bills anywhere. She'd never find it if it was wedged in one of those bundles of hundred or thousand dollar bills. Near the bottom, she felt small, hard blocks, a bunch of them. She pulled one up enough to see a glint of gold.

Just as she was about to give up, her fingertips skated over something hard and plastic. A phone or…? She squeezed until she was able to grab it and pull it out. It was a really small black rectangular box, and she'd bet anything this was the tracker.

She knew exactly what to do with it. Her turmoil helped her scramble to her feet again, walk close to the beaver pond and throw that evil little thing into the water. It hardly made a ripple before sinking.

Then she marched back to the bag, pulled up the zipper and heaved it into her arms. It was a lot heavier than she'd imagined. She wouldn't be able to carry it far, so she had to find an especially good hiding place.

Bri ended up dragging the bag as she all but crawled upward between giant trees. In the few places that were more open, ferns and some kind of bushes formed thickets. With the leaves having fallen, could one of those clumps truly hide the bag? Or was she still too close to the wreckage?

It seemed ages before she almost ran into what at first sight looked like a wall. It was a huge tree, she realized, that had crashed down for some reason.

But then she saw the root mass, and a humongous hole that was filled with shrubs and ferns pushing their way through the tangle of thick roots. Even some tiny trees had grown from seed here. They wouldn't have leaves until spring, but if she could push the bag completely out of sight… A handful of moss dropped after the duffel hid any hint of the silver.

Yes!

Shaking, she faced a larger challenge. Where could *she* hide that they couldn't find *her*?

Too much of the day was gone by the time the helicopter landed. The pilot apologized; she'd had to refuel twice. Once she unloaded her passengers wherever they had chosen, she'd make more passes over territory where the plane could conceivably be.

At first glimpse, Cam was reassured by what he saw of the two law enforcement rangers. They were armed, carrying both sidearms and rifles. One had a coiled rope attached to his pack, as a couple of the others did, including Cam. They wore the classic dark green uniforms, which would help them move unseen, but also gave them the authority to reassure any hikers or climbers the party happened upon. In fact, this was their jurisdiction. Cam wouldn't butt heads over it with them…until they made decisions he disagreed with.

They appeared friendly and seemed to know everyone except Mara, Reggie Davis and Cam. Cam shouted introductions but wasn't sure anyone could hear the names. One of them raised his voice to greet him as Agent Frasier. Cam flicked a glance at Mara to see her gaze moving from him to the ranger and back again. Had she heard?

Damn, he should have told her when they were alone. She'd be mad either way, but the longer he strung this deception out, the more betrayed she'd feel.

After consulting with park service personnel, Cam had agreed with their recommendation that the team be dropped on a ridge top, over 6,700 feet at its highest elevation. He was hoping they'd have as wide a view as possible and had been told that they could descend on the west side without roping off a cliff or serious scrambling. It appeared the two rangers hadn't disagreed with his reasoning. If they saw nothing, not even a sheared-off tree, they could spread out to work their way along any of half a dozen creeks. That was the theory, anyway; since trails were almost nonexistent in this part of the park, the going would be painfully slow. He almost thought *impossible* but wouldn't let himself. They needed to find that wreckage, and they needed to find it soon. For a lot of reasons.

# *Chapter Five*

Bri thought she first heard a small plane, then a while later a helicopter, but she couldn't see either through the deep woods. Were people looking for her yet? Maybe, but how would they know *where* to look? She strained to listen, hoping the helicopter especially would turn back and pass overhead, but it didn't. For just those brief moments, she felt less alone.

Authorities did find small planes that had crashed if someone activated what was called a beacon, but she had no idea what that looked like or how to do it. It almost had to be in the cockpit, didn't it? The way the whole cockpit of the plane had been squished, chances of finding it were zilch, and she wasn't going to climb over Mom and Dennis's dead bodies looking.

What worried her most was that the people who'd shot down Dennis's plane had the best idea where it was. Lots better than any rescuers. Bri would wish *she* knew where she was, except what good would that do?

She had to find the tail of the wrecked plane before dark. Shaking again, she kept looking.

Once, she saw a doe on the other side of the creek. It had been getting a drink; water still dripped off its muzzle as it stared at her. So fast the movement blurred, the doe whirled and ran, disappearing into the green undergrowth as if there was nothing to it. Apparently she had a thick enough coat to be able to ignore nettles, spiny leaves and scratchy branches.

Bri didn't have energy left to feel resentment. She trudged and scrambled her way along. Twice, she slipped on moss-coated rocks and stepped into icy cold water. Now her right foot squished with every step.

If she got much farther and hadn't seen more parts of the airplane, she'd have to turn around and...she didn't quite know. Try to make her way through the huge trees and climb toward the mountains she'd seen through the window before everything went wrong. Otherwise, what if some parts of the plane had been flung onto the other side of the creek? That was possible, wasn't it? She started being more careful scanning that way, too.

So tired she didn't know if she could keep going, for a moment Bri thought she was imagining it when she saw just a sliver of white beyond a big boulder that the creek seemed to curve around. Heart pounding, she tried to hurry and immediately slipped on moss and fell to her knees. It hurt, but then all of her hurt.

She pushed herself up, wobbled and persuaded one of her legs to go forward. Then the other one. She had to concentrate so fiercely, it was almost a shock to bump right into the boulder. Already she could see that there was a large part of the plane behind it.

"Please," she whispered again. "Please, please, please."

The first thing she saw was another seat, this one twisted and poking out over the stream. It made no sense for it to still be attached to the rear section of the plane, but there it was. The tail of the plane lay sideways, and she could see into the luggage compartment. It made her mad that she started to cry, but she knew she was lucky this section hadn't been flung somewhere she'd never find. Or into the water.

Without something warm to put on and food, any kind of food, she might die, she knew. She bet it would be cold tonight, and all she had on were ripped leggings and a thin sweatshirt.

And then there were her wet feet.

Careful to avoid jagged pieces of metal, she leaned into the compartment and pulled out bags. She'd go through all of them and decide what was worth carrying and what wasn't. She started with her own, so she could hastily strip and pull on jeans, dry socks and her hiking boots as well as a tank top and dry sweatshirt. Thank goodness she'd brought her parka. Toothbrush and toothpaste, hairbrush, yes. She hadn't brought shampoo, figuring she could use Mom's. Didn't matter, because she wouldn't be taking a shower any time soon.

She opened a rubber tub next and saw a parka even heavier than hers on top. Below it was a rolled blanket, a small plastic box with the Red Cross insignia on it— she definitely wanted that—and finally several unopened boxes of energy bars and a big mixed bag of candy bars, the little ones that they gave out to trick-or-treaters on Halloween.

Bri tore that one open right away and gobbled two candy bars without even paying attention to what they were until she dropped the wrappers: Butterfinger and Snickers.

Mom's suitcase next. Mom was taller than Bri and, well, shaped differently, but Bri could wear some of her clothes. Everything was packed super neatly, but Bri just pulled stuff out and tossed what she didn't want. What difference did it make? A wool sweater was a yes, a pair of thin leather gloves, great, extra socks and a knit hat. Where did Mom think they were going, the arctic?

At the bottom, she found a photo album. Her heart cramped. Even though she should hurry, she paged through it, seeing mostly pictures of her, some of Dad, some of all of them. By the time she closed it, she realized she was crying. She hated leaving it, but she put it back in the bottom of the suitcase, crammed some of Mom's stuff back in and carefully zipped it up, putting it back in the luggage compartment. Maybe rescuers would take the personal things like this and give them back to Bri.

If she lived. And she wouldn't if she didn't hurry.

So that was what she did, deciding as best she could what mattered and what didn't. She ended up using the duffel bag that had had Dennis's clothes before she dumped them out, because hers was made out of canvas with swirls of purple and pink, and somehow she didn't think Mom's suitcase would roll along beside her through the wilderness.

The last thing she did was tug Mom's hat on her head, even if it was a brighter color than she liked, stick the gloves in the kangaroo pocket of her sweatshirt, and figure out how she could carry the duffel bag sort of like a backpack instead of over one shoulder.

Then she followed tracks probably made by deer, or whatever other animals lived here, and started walking.

She was deep under the trees when she heard a helicopter. This time she was sure that was what it was. She went still, leaning on the trunk of a tree, and listened hard. If it came close enough, did she dare go out into the open and wave her hands? Or if it landed, could she hide fast to see who got out?

If Aunt Mara wasn't with them, or anyone Bri recognized from Thunder Creek, should she show herself?

Thinking about that tracker, if that was what it was, Bri thought the helicopter wouldn't have arrived so close to the crash site this fast unless it had been sent by the same men who'd shot Dennis and the airplane a few times until it went down.

No, she had to get as far away as she could and then hide.

THE PILOT OF the park service helicopter somehow found a spot free enough of rocks and heavy growth to allow her to set it down so they could more easily unload. The pilot waved Cam to her as the others hefted their packs and jumped out, running bent over until they were beyond the rotors.

She pulled off her headphones and yelled, "Saw another helicopter. Probably sightseers. I wish I'd been able to get a better look."

"Where was it?"

She waved south. He'd give a lot to know whether it was in fact carrying tourists willing to pay well for an up-close view of the jagged Picket Range, or whether it was the suspected traffickers arrowing in on where they knew Terrell's plane had gone down.

She said she'd continue her search route and call on the SAT radio if she saw anything. Thinking of the plane that had apparently driven Terrell's down into this rugged territory, he told her to be careful and jumped to the ground.

He winced a little at the stress on muscles and a long-ago war wound, joined the others and waved goodbye to the helicopter as it rose and circled east.

The team gathered around him, waiting for instructions. It seemed to him that Mara hung back a little. She wasn't the only one who apparently had reservations about his ability to lead them.

"The pilot just told me she spotted another helicopter but didn't get a good enough look to identify it. It was south, this side of the Pickets. Instead of trying to follow it, she plans to take up where she left off earlier in her search grid."

Several members nodded.

"Quite a view from here, but I'd hoped we could get a better look into the valleys. I guess for the bird's eye view, we'll have to depend on the pilot. This morning I spoke to a couple of folks who've been in charge of searches here and in the Olympics. They seem confident that if the plane had come down on ice or rock, fly-bys would spot it. Likewise, it should have done some visible damage to trees if it hit a heavily wooded area. Which suggests creek valleys, beneath a rock overhang or low where the trees are small enough to have softened the landing but are either flexible or thin enough to allow a plane the size of the one we're looking for to pass through. Unfortunately, as you all know, the growth is so thick, we won't be able to move as fast as I'd like. Were any of you able to bring a machete or the like?"

Four hands raised.

"Good. I have one, too. When we have to spread out, I suggest we keep who has one in mind."

"Why are we *here*?" Mara asked. "What do you expect we can see that wasn't visible from a helicopter?"

"This ridge is central to the likely search area, and the pilot preferred to land the helicopter instead of having to lower us by rope. We're all equipped with binoculars. Let's use them frequently. Once we've descended from the ridge, we'll break up into pairs. As I'm sure you're all aware, we only have a few hours before sunset. It's too dangerous to stumble on in the dark."

The doctor frowned. "We rarely stop at night. I assume we all have headlamps...?"

The general agreement didn't surprise Cam, but he said, "The chances are good we're not alone out here. A string of lights would make us dangerously visible. I don't like the idea of settling down for a good night's sleep any better than you do, but we have to remain as unseen as we can manage. Also, this is tough terrain, and it may take us multiple days to find the crash site."

He waited, but nobody argued. Lowering his pack to the ground, he pulled out a map of the area from Mount Shuksan to just beyond the daunting Picket Range and south toward Ross Lake. Everybody gathered closer.

"The first caller, who was climbing Mt. Baker, lost sight of the plane behind Shuksan." They were almost directly east of Shuksan now. He described where the second caller had been when she saw the plane go down. "I think our bull's-eye is in this location." He tapped the surrounding creek valleys and drainages: Baker, Picket, Bald Eagle leading down to Lonesome Creek. "This seems most logical to me. Doesn't mean we won't have to adjust north or southeast."

"West?" the male deputy asked.

He decided that wasn't a challenge. "Conceivable, but that would take us closer to some trails that could have hikers on them in October, especially with the good weather." He shrugged. "If any of you had better ideas, I assume you would have shared them. Or still would." Silence. "By tomorrow, we might call in more searchers. It's also possible we may not be able to locate the wreckage until some climber stumbles on it next spring. Right now, our emphasis is on rescue. Don't put yourself at risk, though. Watch for anyone else beating the bushes in search of the same crash site."

He'd gone over much of this previously during individual phone calls as well as once they gathered. There'd been no pushback. Now, they all glanced around with new uneasiness, then nodded again.

"At least one in each pair has a SAT phone." Cell phones rarely worked in Washington's three mountainous national parks. Even the radios might not work when calling from one side of a high ridge to the other. "If you see anything worth exploring or worrisome, call it in."

Initially leaving their packs in a heap, they spread out along a ridge that he personally would have called a mountain even if it didn't rise to a sharp peak like Mount Fury or Mount Challenger and lacked any obvious remnant of a glacier or year-round snow. This was some of the roughest country in the US, all sharp ups and downs.

Cam hadn't said how unlikely he thought it was that they'd stumble on pieces of an airplane that hadn't been all that large. The best bet had been from eyes in the sky, seeing slashed trunks or branches or even evidence of a fire. He could only thank God rain had fallen a few days ago. The devastation just north along the Chilliwack showed what could happen—and September and October were relatively dry months here until snow started to fall in mid to late November.

While he was feeling thankful, he should also be glad this hadn't happened a couple of months from now, when searchers would have to rely on snowshoes even in what limited areas they could access.

He wasn't surprised that Mara had disappeared with Cardoza, the doctor, while Joe Walden, the climber, had joined Cam. Cam would definitely be making some changes before they split up more permanently, and he was getting the feeling that Mara wouldn't like it.

He was also well aware that this was confession time, before he and she crawled into a tent together…or he succumbed to the temptation of kissing her.

"YOU HAVE DOUBTS about this guy?" Daniel jerked his head the direction Cam had gone.

"I probably shouldn't," Mara admitted, "but there's an awful lot I don't know about him. He was just assigned to Thunder Creek two weeks ago. I assumed he wasn't new to the sheriff's department, but Lori didn't know him. I'm not sure she even knows Reggie Davis, but they might work different shifts, different parts of the county. Frasier may have just hired on with Whatcom County, but I'm puzzled as to why he was sent to an isolated posting right away."

And why, she asked herself, had he somehow avoided

answering any questions about his background when they were supposedly spending an evening together?

Or maybe she should ask herself why she hadn't pushed a little harder. *All I knew was that he was too good to be true*, she thought ruefully. And really, what was *her* excuse for not telling him her relevant background?

"He sounds like he's used to giving orders," the doctor commented.

"I agree." She hesitated. "I assume he's done search and rescue somewhere, but if it was here in the north Cascades, you'd think one of us would have met or heard of him. All he's said is that he was army and deployed a few times."

Daniel glanced at her. "That's not so different."

"No." She lifted her binoculars and scanned until her eyes burned, then let them fall from the strap around her neck. "Shouldn't the park service be calling the shots? Does the national transportation safety board know about this crash? Aren't they all over even small plane crashes?"

He shook his head. "Don't know."

Mara made herself shut up. Undermining Cam's authority wouldn't be smart, especially since she couldn't dispute his choices so far, however desperate she'd been to get going the moment she heard about the crash. She couldn't imagine she'd sleep a wink tonight, knowing Bri was out there somewhere, maybe hurt, cold, terrified. Mara didn't let herself think about the alternative.

When their group gathered again, all shaking heads, Cam said, "The park service pilot let me know she didn't see anything out of the ordinary and is on her way back to base. She's running low on fuel and daylight." That wasn't a surprise. "Let's start our descent. Have any of you hiked in this area?"

Joe lifted a hand. "I've been up several of the mountains in the Picket Range. Heck, several of you have done rescues on those mountains with me."

Almost all of them had hiked here in the Cascade National Park but on established trails. Reggie, stocky and appearing strong, was likely the most recent transplant to the northwest corner of the state, aside from Cam.

Packs on their backs, they began what turned out to be a tough descent from the ridge. It included a tiny lake and one drop-off so steep, even Joe called it a class three pitch, which nobody would choose for a hike. The category meant seriously steep, but not a complete drop-off.

Near the end, they could hear water, apparently a fork of the Baker River watershed. Nature grew more junglelike, except the deciduous trees that mixed with the ubiquitous cedar, fir, hemlock and spruce were mostly leafless. An occasional red or orange leaf clung precariously to a twig here and there. Earlier in the year, they might have been able to pick huckleberries, but the fruit was gone along with the leaves that would have identified the bushes.

The opposite side of the river rose even more steeply than the ridge behind them. Mara knew from studying the map that this creek drained snowmelt from Mineral Mountain.

They dropped their packs and took a break, sitting on a fallen log or rocks.

"Okay," Cam said, "I'm going to ask a couple of you to head north on Mineral Creek until it peters out, then see where you can reach from there. The rest of us will start south until we meet Picket Creek. From there, some will go west on Baker River, then northwest on Pass Creek, others east in the Picket Creek valley."

Everyone listened carefully; their rescues usually involved lost or injured climbers or hikers, not downed airplanes.

Reggie spoke up. "Why don't you let Mara and me take that southern route? Heading up toward Shuksan looks like the toughest route. I'm not an experienced climber. You might be a stronger partner for Walden."

As if the jerk knew a thing a thing about her. Mara bristled but managed to keep her mouth shut.

"Why did Hayden send you if you have zero climbing experience?" Cam asked scathingly.

The very question Mara had been asking herself. Why had this guy been accepted as a volunteer at all if he wasn't competent in precipitous drops and the complicated riggings required in many rescues?

Reggie flushed with anger. "I didn't say that—"

"Mara knows this country better than you do." Cam swept the group with a gaze while completely dismissing Reggie and his opinion.

Dark color on his cheeks, Reggie glared at their leader.

Mara couldn't help feeling sorry for whoever ended up being paired with him.

No give in his voice, Cam added, "Stay in touch. I think it makes sense for park service to pair up. Otherwise, sheriff's deputies, split up. Deputy Holmes, you go with Dr. Cardoza, Davis, you sound like you need Joe's expertise. Try not to slow him down. Mara, you'll stay with me. That way, one member of each pair is armed, just in case."

Did that mean he saw her as a weak link? Or had he chosen the route for the two of them that he thought likeliest to be the crash site? Despite her mixed feelings where he was concerned, she was glad to stay with him. Maybe it was that air of sheer competency. Also, she found herself liking Reggie less by the minute. He was still glowering, his shoulders hunched like he wanted to launch himself at Cam. Fortunately for him, he didn't say another word.

She switched her gaze to Cam. If he saw her as more vulnerable than the rest, she'd have to enlighten him soon. Accompanying the thought, her right hand touched the holster of the handgun she wore at her hip, unseen.

*Focus on Bri*, she told herself. This was no time to think about her attraction to this mysterious man or his secrets.

# Chapter Six

So little daylight remained, Cam felt chagrined that he hadn't suggested camping atop the ridge where there was at least some open ground. Here, masses of ferns and other low-growing stems and branches of unknown shrubs grew out of moss-covered ground and rotting logs and stumps of long-fallen forest giants. A broken ankle waiting to happen. Even so, no one here would have welcomed a traditional, leisurely stop for the night. They needed to cover as much ground as they could.

He'd have liked to have some privacy to talk to Mara, but from the map, the closest to level ground they'd find would be during the short stretch before Mineral Creek reached Baker River where most of them would split up.

Without suggesting they stop, the two park rangers split with the rest of the party after very few words. Cam winced, seeing the pinched V cut by Mineral Creek. He wouldn't want to try to beat his way along it and could only imagine the difficulty during the spring when snowmelt would flood it.

The rest of them turned south, spreading out in the difficult terrain. The members of the group scrambled over boulders, slipped on the ubiquitous moss that lay like a bright green carpet with the texture of velvet, disguising the myriad traps it covered. Cam would have expected it to be brown, too, but this had been a particularly rainy spring that cut the summer short.

Cam wrenched an ankle almost immediately, swore under his breath and kept going. Ahead of him, Mara moved with surprising grace, sure-footed. She made him think of a doe with those long, slender legs and dainty feet, never so much as hesitating. Luck had chanced to put Mara in the lead, except he kept finding himself watching her instead of his surroundings. Probably best that the bulk of her pack and the dangling bundle of rope hid most of her figure.

He scowled at the direction of his thoughts.

He'd hiked a handful of times in the north Cascades since he was transferred to the Seattle office of the FBI, but that hadn't been enough to give him any useful familiarity with this overgrown wilderness. This wouldn't be like search and rescue in almost any other part of the world. He shouldn't have assumed he could handle anything. What bothered him most was wondering what Mara thought about him, a big, clumsy brute, crashing along behind her.

And there he went again.

Since she'd been in the lead, she was the one to stop their whole group with one lifted hand.

"Bear."

It didn't have the distinctive hump of a grizzly, so the bear that stood knee deep in the water had to be a black bear, although this one was cinnamon colored. To Cam's eyes, it was enormous, the head massive. It only stared at them from beady eyes.

"Shoo!" Mara called, waving her arms over her head.

The bear was not impressed.

Joe, who was just behind Cam, said, "Why don't we just cut uphill a little ways and circle by?"

Someone farther back mumbled, "Can't be much worse."

Mara apparently agreed, because she veered slightly away from the creek. The land wasn't steep, but the tangle of vegetation that grew between the rocks tried to swallow them. Whippy branches slashed at Cam, as if irritated that he dared push his way among them. The bear, thank God, only watched them go.

Once Mara paused long enough to point at a particularly nasty looking shrub and said, "Devil's club. It has a few leaves left on it. Try not to let those barbs get near your face or hands."

As he had just discovered a clump of the leaves, he clamped his mouth shut and didn't say anything. Blast it, that hurt!

Even with the sun lowering fast, he was sweating and gave brief thought to shedding his quarter-zip until they stopped for the night, but that would have left his arms bare. What excused the creation of such a vicious addition to the vegetation?

"Normally," she added over her shoulder, "I'd tell you to watch for the nettles, too, but you probably recognize those."

He grimaced and got himself moving again.

Within moments, they lost sight of the sky. The dense evergreen forest reached high. Cam found himself using the rough trunks to push himself upright. Occasional lower-growing cedar branches made for good handholds.

He'd have said no sunlight at all reached them, but

he noticed when the light dimmed. Mara aimed slightly downhill, until he heard the soft ripple of the water again. Then she stopped and looked right past him.

"Joe, what do you think? This as good as it's going to get?"

Joe Walden, undoubtedly the most experienced at travel in this remarkable, mountainous rainforest, advanced to Cam's side and studied what Cam would not have described as a clearing. "I think so. We don't dare stumble on into dusk, even if we were sure we were alone. Somebody will get hurt." He glanced at Cam. "Up to you."

"No," Cam said ruefully, "I'm not the expert in this back country." Iraq, Afghanistan, yes. Even a memorable chase in the Rocky Mountains. He'd undoubtedly been shot at more than anyone else in this party, but he didn't recall ever having to swipe long, lacy strands of what he assumed was lichen off his face.

"Lucky it doesn't look like rain," Joe said briskly.

"Hey, at this time of year, none of us brought tents anyway," Mara remarked.

Joe's grin was downright puckish, crinkling skin beside his eyes and mouth. "You can't believe the blue sky when you're surrounded by mountains the way we are."

Mountains? What mountains? Not as if they could see so much as the sharp point of any of the Picket Range.

"That's what tarps are for," she said cheerfully.

Unwilling to betray his relative ignorance, Cam turned and raised his voice. "We're going to set up camp here as well as we can and wait for daylight to go on."

The only one who looked surprised was Reggie Davis, the deputy who'd admitted to moving to Washington recently. Oregon had plenty of forests, but from what Cam had read they tended to be drier than this and growing out of gentler slopes.

As they shuffled around trying to find relatively level spots, somehow Mara slipped by him and joined Lori Holmes, which Cam grudgingly conceded made sense. Neither woman would probably feel comfortable snuggling down to sleep with a near stranger who happened to be male.

Joe and the doctor ended up side by side, too, which again made sense, as they'd likely known each other for years. Cam's chosen spot had enough moss to seem surprisingly comfortable after he'd set down his pack, spread his pad and sleeping bag and sat down. He leaned back against a good-size trunk and shifted to scratch his back. At least the trunk would keep him from rolling on down to the creek if he slept too deeply.

He had to look around for Davis, seeing him noticeably separate from the group as well. Might just be flattest place he'd been able to find. But Cam caught the deputy studying the others, his gaze moving slowly from face to face, as if he were assessing each and every one of them. Maybe natural, maybe not. After all, Cam was doing the same thing, assessing in particular the one outsider in this group.

*The one outsider besides me*, he thought, not sure how he felt about that. No question, he'd be more relaxed with known teammates. The two park rangers he had trouble even picturing, so brief had been their inclusion. He was mildly surprised to realize he'd let go of some of his usual wariness for the three members of the group it was clear Mara knew and trusted. And for her, of course.

Davis's eyes met his at that moment, and the two men stared at each other. Finally, Cam tipped his head in some kind of acknowledgment, even as he tried to decide why he felt uneasy about a fellow lawman.

HAD CAM GOTTEN on his radio to report their location to anyone? Mara didn't think so. Although really, what would have been the point? They hadn't gotten very far.

Stressed enough not to be hungry, she nibbled on nuts and dried fruit instead of setting up her camp stove. Were they even *close* to Bri? In this vast wilderness, the odds of one of eight people happening to stumble on her were ludicrously low, even if Cam and the park service rangers had done their best to guess where the plane had gone down.

If Bri had survived, what were the chances she had anything to eat? What if she was hurt or even trapped in the wreckage? What if… Mara sucked in a breath. This kind of thinking was no help at all.

Bri would know someone was coming for her. Mara had gone on a two-day rescue only a few weeks after she moved to Thunder Creek. A man in his forties had had a heart attack. He had been shocked, although he admitted to not exercising regularly, not having traveled much above sea level in years, and, yeah, he was carrying some extra pounds as well as an enormous pack.

Mara had told Bri about her SAR teammates, about the distraught wife who'd held her husband's hand whenever the trail was wide enough for her to walk beside him.

Mara closed her eyes. *We're coming, honey. Have faith.*

She was the one who needed to have faith, but right now that was a struggle. She wished she had sat down closer to Cam, who had heated a freeze-dried meal, cleaned up efficiently afterward, and was now talking to Deputy Davis, who nodded a few times but didn't seem to be saying much. Then Cam moved on, stopping to check on each one of them. A natural leader, which came as no surprise to her.

He squatted to talk to Joe and Dr. Cardoza, listening this time and nodding. Smart enough to accept advice from experts. That didn't surprise her, either.

He rose as if he didn't feel a twinge from this afternoon's effort, never mind having been awakened at an ungodly hour this morning. When he reached Lori and Mara, he lowered himself to his haunches again, resting his forearms on powerful thighs. "Get enough to eat?"

Even in the fading light, she could tell he was looking at her.

"Sure."

He raised his eyebrows at Lori, who said cheerfully, "I would have shared with Mara if she'd been hungry enough."

"Okay." His gaze flicked upward to a bat that darted overhead. "It's so gloomy under here, we may not even notice when the sun has really set or when dawn arrives."

It was hard to make out Lori's face. "Fires outside of designated campgrounds aren't allowed in the park no matter what. Too bad. I miss camping with my folks and roasting marshmallows."

Mara actually felt herself smile. "You mean burning them?"

Lori grinned. "Most of the time."

"You okay with the pairing for tomorrow?" he asked Lori.

She assured him she was. "You have a good group here. I'm fine with either Joe or Dan."

Cam didn't ask Mara the same question. In a way, it made sense to pair each woman with a man who had greater bulk and strength. Also, Mara would have been uncomfortable with Reggie, a complete stranger. But it was more than that; something told her that Reggie wouldn't have been willing to accede to her greater knowledge about these mountains.

She might not feel as if she really knew Cam, but he was familiar and, for no reason she could put her finger on, reassuring. She especially needed reassurance. Mara had been on enough rescues that she would have said she understood how the family of the missing or injured felt. But right this minute, she realized her empathy had never plunged into the true depths of terror for a loved one.

Cam stood again, looked down at the two women for a minute, then said, "Get some rest."

She and Lori took turns slipping into the darkness and taking care of business before unzipping their sleeping bags and squirming into them.

"Ugh," Lori mumbled. "There's a tree root right under my butt."

"Scoot over my way."

The other woman did, wriggled a little, then said, "That's better."

"'Night."

A few other quiet words were exchanged, an owl

hooted before swooping low over them, and Mara strained to hear any other sound at all.

Mara tried to breathe slowly, deeply, to relax. Her fingernails bit into her palms. She *had* to get some sleep. For Bri's sake. Fear and grief kept her awake, anyway, staring up at darkness.


Hand flat on the rough trunk of some kind of tree, Bri forced herself to lift her left foot. It didn't want to go. She hadn't known it was possible to be so tired, to hurt so much, she didn't know if she could move another inch. Of if she should, with no light at all.

Anyway, it wasn't as if she had a goal or had been moving very fast. All she'd been thinking was *away*. Once, hours ago, she had heard voices. Or imagined them. Who knew? What if they'd been rescuers? What if one of them was Aunt Mara? Except a woman's voice sounded different, and the few words Bri had caught had been from men, she was sure of that.

She tried to move her right foot. When nothing happened, she let herself crumple to the ground, her only anchor the big tree scraping her hand as she dropped. The straps of the duffel bag slipped off her shoulder, and it fell, too, panicking her until she was able to grope and find it.

She wished she had the sleeping bag, but it had been too bulky. She'd discarded other stuff that might turn out to be important, but she couldn't even remember what she had and what she didn't.

Instead of unzipping the bag, she curled up on her side, grateful for the moss and for the texture of the tree trunk at her back. She wrapped her arms around the mostly soft duffel bag, as if it was Aunt Mara, except Aunt Mara would have talked gently to her until she fell asleep.

Bri didn't believe she *could* sleep, but just lying down like this was a huge relief.

A rustle in the darkness made her stiffen. She stared wildly but saw nothing. After that, she couldn't relax again. There wasn't any part of her body that didn't hurt. Her head throbbed, and her muscles ached. Sharp pains struck her middle every time she breathed. One knee hurt more than everything else put together.

After a while, she started to shiver. She made herself open the duffel bag and find first the parka, then the blanket. Her teeth chattered as she pulled on the parka. Once she zipped the duffel back up, she used it as a pillow and tried to burrow inside the blanket, like a small animal hiding from nighttime predators.

Maybe in the morning, she'd be able to plan. Except she kind of doubted it. When she regained consciousness that morning, she hadn't been able to see the only landmark she'd have recognized, Mount Shuksan. As terrified as she'd been, all the zigzagging that Dennis had done meant she could be anywhere.

Bri desperately wanted to be home… No, she couldn't think about her mother. At Aunt Mara's, then, cuddled in the guest bedroom that was really Bri's.

She drifted in her head, started fully awake, then gave up and welcomed the darkness.

# Chapter Seven

The sky was still a shimmery gray with dawn when the group reached Picket Creek where Lori Holmes and Daniel Cardoza were to break off to explore the curving creek that flowed with snowmelt from the high ridges on each side. Fortunately, none of the creeks ran as high as they would have in early summer. At least on the map, the headwaters of this one formed between Mount Crowder, part of the Picket Range, and Pioneer Ridge. Of course, distances on a map weren't as telling as the elevation climb or plunge. After they reached the head of the creek, they intended to do some scrambling in hopes of finding a way to cut cross-country.

All six of them had to splash across the creek before they continued because of the cliff rising on the north side of the valley. Mara trailed Cam, trying to step from rock to rock, but when his larger foot slipped into the water with a splash, she was distracted. Of course, she stepped on a rock that rolled underfoot. The water was *cold.*

Already across with dry feet, Lori looked smug, while the doctor said, "Be aware if you start getting a blister because of wet socks."

Great advice. Lori laughed at everyone else's expressions.

Apparently deciding to ignore any discomfort, Cam said, "After dropping another group of searchers well south from us, the helicopter will be flying a grid again. Chances are good we'll see it."

They all agreed to stay in touch. Mara had overheard Cam talking to Joe this morning, so she knew Reggie and Joe would split off to follow a creek that flowed from the foot of Shuksan—tough country. Of all of them, Joe was the most experienced with real rock climbing. Reggie? At least he appeared muscular and strong. Would he follow the experienced climber's instructions? Who knew?

Cam intended for Mara and him to head south on yet another part of the drainage not long after the party split. He'd felt Baker River itself was open enough to be visible from the air, and soon reached a trail that might still have hikers at this time of year. He didn't believe the plane could have entirely disappeared that close to Baker Lake and the Baker River trail.

She'd memorized the map well enough to agree with Cam's reasoning, even if he had to know that the map could be outdated. For example, fallen timber or rocks could block a stream or even a river, making a route essentially unpassable. The wildfire that had decimated the Copper Ridge area, now closed to hikers and climbers, was a lesson. It hadn't been noted on the map they were using.

She listened but heard only the ripple of the creek. No girl's voice. By the time she got moving, a decent distance had opened up between her and the other two. Right away, she discovered that she *felt* Cam in a way she didn't anyone else. It was like an itch between her shoulder blades. Maybe he'd step on her heel any minute. She finally surrendered to the impulse to sneak a look over her shoulder.

He was a comfortable distance behind her.

He must have seen her peek back, because he asked, "You get any sleep?"

She opened her mouth with the full intention of telling a lie, then closed it, settling for, "Not much."

"Lucky to find a game trail," he observed, not commenting on her admission. "Keep your fingers crossed it doesn't peter out a few hundred yards from now."

He was right. Between the tumbled rocks and the low, snarled roots of alder and willow, it was miraculous to be able to walk without bushwhacking for even a short while. Without comment, she kept an eye on Reggie—or, really, his huge pack—and tried to pretend she wasn't still so painfully conscious of Cam behind her.

In the V of this valley, she couldn't see the Pickets but knew the sharp-toothed mountain range wasn't far away. Mount Challenger, Mount Fury, Phantom Peak were just a few of the jagged mountains that she prayed the small plane hadn't crashed into. If so, there was no hope at all.

About the time the trail disappeared, the four of them took a break. They all sat in a row on a good-size tree that hadn't been down long enough for moss to crawl over it and begin the process of decay.

"Where is that helicopter?" The edge in Cam's voice was noticeable.

Joe leaned forward to look around Reggie. "We got a really early start."

"While the pilot slept in?" Cam grimaced. "I know

better than that. She had to collect the other searchers. I shouldn't be impatient. She'd be doing well to get in the air again by now."

Mara's tension reached such a peak, she was about to jump to her feet and start out whether everybody else was ready or not. Forestalling her, Joe stretched, rose and set out, his confidence showing. Reggie stuck close to him. Mara wished she could split herself to be able to see what all of the others, including the helicopter pilot, saw. If—no, *when*—someone came upon the crash site, how much lag time would there be before she heard? How many miles away might she be by then?

*Pay attention to what you're doing*, she ordered herself. She needed to concentrate on where she set down each foot so she didn't trip. Carelessness could lead her to grab a spiny branch for balance, leaving her with a painful rash for hours. Or, worse, trip and break an ankle. There was a pause ahead.

Joe took out a machete and started whacking a path. A short time later, Reggie took a turn. When she judged it was her turn, Cam stepped past her and shook his head.

"We have upper body strength you don't. With three of us, we can move as fast as possible."

Mara never liked being told she couldn't do something, but in this case…he was right. She'd never used a machete, which meant she'd have been in danger of slicing a leg off. Besides, while she had endurance on the move, her upper arms weren't even half as thick with muscle as Cam's were.

She'd have her chance, say, to wriggle through an opening no one else could.

With them moving slower, she swiveled her head,

trying to see every direction. Any flicker of color, any quiver of branches, but nothing nearby bore any resemblance to a piece of metal machine.

When Cam dropped back again after handing the machete back to Joe, his gaze rested on Mara's face. "I know this pace must be killing you. I'm sorry. This'll be my fault if it turns out they came down outside the circle I drew on the map."

Mara had to struggle before she could respond with any fairness. "You had to make a decision with limited information. No matter what—" Her voice broke. "You couldn't have done any better without X-ray vision."

"Thank you for saying that," he said.

Feeling as if her chest were being crushed by her fear and grief, she needed to know why he'd been in charge from the beginning, but this was hardly the time to ask.

What had to be two hours later, they reached the latest creek tumbling into the Baker River. It wasn't as clear as the others they'd seen thus far.

Joe stared down at the water. "Even this far away, it's getting fouled with ash." His face tightened. "That was the prettiest country."

The fire had decimated a large section of ancient forest long before Mara moved to Thunder Creek. Coming from Bellingham on the Puget Sound, none of the rescues she'd been called out on had taken her to that northern stretch of the Cascade National Park. She'd seen the devastation wrought by fires before, though, and understood that Joe was mourning.

They took a last break together before hefting their packs again, slapping hands and separating. Pass Creek was an ironic name for a route that easily could prove to be impassible. She didn't linger to watch Joe and Reggie go, though. Instead, she said, "We should cross here."

She made it without slipping this time, but Cam stepped with the same foot into the river, swearing as he cleared the bank.

"Hear that?"

Mara cocked her head. "The helicopter!" She turned in place. "That's southeast, I think." Farther away than the current search party would be able to cover. Looking up at the limitless arch of blue sky made her feel smaller, less hopeful.

Cam had turned with her. "She'll let us know if she sees something."

He wouldn't have bothered to say something so unnecessary if he hadn't felt the need to reassure her. She must not be hiding her emotions as well as she'd thought she was.

Brief gratitude didn't do much to quell her bone-deep fear. "Will she be able to come back tomorrow, too?"

"I hope so. Today—" His massive pack moved as he rolled his shoulders. "I don't know how far she'll get before she needs to refuel."

He dug his machete out of his pack, then set out.

THEIR PACE SLOWED drastically from that point. The rampant growth in the low V between the steep ridges and mountains didn't surprise Mara, but she'd never been so desperate to hurry before, so afraid. Even the leafless growth knotted into traps.

No game trail here. Cam used his machete for a while, but that meant each stride forward took a minute or more. Looking down, Mara pictured a cat's cradle made out of string, except there was no discernable pattern. Despite his effort, she kept having to wrench her booted feet out of brown snares or catch herself from tumbling down. A fall would be devastating. What if the helicopter had to rescue *her*? If her own mistake meant she couldn't be here for Bri?

They reached a stretch where it initially felt easier to clamber from boulder to boulder than doing battle with vegetation. Cam invariably stepped from one to another or sometimes jumped, and then reached back to catch her hand.

With their progress so agonizingly slow, Mara was startled when he said, "Let's take a lunch break."

Lunch? How could the sun have risen so high without her awareness? "I'm not really hungry."

"We have to keep our strength up."

He was right, of course. Mara was beginning to be annoyed at how often she had to think that. "Yes. Okay."

He led her to a suitable flat-topped rock that allowed them to sit and slide out of their backpacks. Her muscles groaned in relief, but in her anxiety all she wanted to do was put the blasted thing back on so they could keep going.

She stayed put, though, and they both dug in their packs, producing a variety of packets of dried fruit, nuts and granola. Mara took a long drink of water before she popped some peanuts in her mouth.

Cam gazed pensively across the creek as he followed suit. She bit her lip, studying his strong profile. When better to ask the questions that had choked her ever since they set out yesterday morning? "You think it'll be your fault if we don't find the crash site."

The hand reaching for his own water bottle paused before he said, "Who else is there to blame?"

"I don't know. I mean, *somebody* had to make decisions. What I keep wondering is, why was it you? Shouldn't park rangers have been in charge?"

He tipped his head back as if to study the dense forest and solid rock of the ridge that reared on the other side of the creek. Or to avoid answering her question. Finally, he rolled his shoulders and turned his head to meet her eyes. "I'm not a Whatcom County deputy. The sheriff's department gave me cover to investigate the new resort and everyone associated with it." The muscles in his jaw flexed. "I'm an FBI agent."

"*What?*" In one way she was shocked, in another… not. Something about this man and the role he'd assumed had never felt right. "Why?"

"Why are we investigating? The money consortium behind this resort is made up of people who have already built a similar one in Southern California, close to the Mexican border. Both were built in relatively remote places and were or are promoted for their private runways and hangars. There are plenty of rich people who like being able to fly their own planes when they vacation. Those strips are also handy if you're wanting to move people or drugs across the border without drawing a lot of attention."

"People?"

"Human trafficking is still a problem. We think Levin and his partners are primarily associated with a drug cartel. Other agents are investigating the California resort. We don't have enough evidence for warrants, and at this stage wouldn't find anything if we crawled all over this resort. Not until it's up and running. We tried to get agents hired by the contractor but failed. Thunder Creek is too remote, too small, for strangers not to stand out."

Oh, *he'd* stood out, all right.

"It turned out to be convenient that Deputy Walker was about to be traded out for a replacement."

Not for a minute did she forget Bri, but underneath that fear bubbled a stew of emotions: anger, betrayal, hurt… Oh, that was just the beginning. "You were mostly interested in Dennis, weren't you?" Ice skimmed her voice. "No wonder you latched right on to me. How better to keep tabs on Dennis, get a sense of his character, hear any news about him."

"That's how it started." He sounded gruff. "I hadn't spent an hour with you when I regretted that. I'm… I like you. You have to believe that much."

"Most men can work up some interest in almost any woman. And when she turns out to be so useful—"

"If I'd met you anywhere else, any other time, I'd still have asked you out."

"Uh-huh. So am I the only one along on this jaunt who didn't know you're really Special Agent Frasier?"

"No." He sounded hoarse. "Just the park rangers and the helicopter pilot knew. Your coordinator, too—Bill Hayden."

Her mouth twisted. "No wonder everyone jumped when you snapped your fingers. I suppose you had no trouble getting the cooperation of the border patrol or the Canadians monitoring air space or—"

"Stop." Creases appeared on his forehead, and the lines between his nose and mouth were crevasses. "I'm doing my job. Hurting you is the last thing I intended. Think about this… What if I hadn't been here, ready to move in a way no one else would have? Who'd have acted? Border patrol?" His voice descended to a growl. "They'd have had no reason to believe this had anything to do with them. FAA? Maybe, if there was convincing evidence that a plane really *had* crashed and the site located. Whatcom County? They have no jurisdiction in the national park. The head ranger admitted they'd never before mounted a search for a plane crash. Who could have acted faster, convinced everybody to fall in line?" He leaned toward her.

Mara refused to shrink back. What right did he have to be angry she'd questioned him? She had no family but for the people on that plane, even if Brianna was the only one she wanted to claim. "It ever occur to you that the people behind that resort suspected you weren't what you appeared to be?" She didn't like her own snappish tone but didn't care. "What if they decided to clean house so you wouldn't find anything? Dennis drank too much, which made him a weak link. Maybe they wouldn't have forced his plane down if it weren't for *you*."

His narrowed, glittering eyes told her how dangerous this man was, even if she hadn't already suspected. She wrenched her own gaze away long enough to see every bone and sinew showing on the backs of his big hands.

In contrast, he spoke quietly. "Do you really believe that?"

Mara hugged herself. She'd have rocked if the bulk of her pack didn't make that impossible. Finally, she moistened her lips and whispered, "No. I…understand you're doing your job. But I hate being lied to." Being used. She shouldn't react this way; it wasn't as if they'd had any kind of meaningful relationship. But he'd acted as if he wanted one, and somehow had slipped beneath her guard. Didn't it figure their acquaintance had begun with a gigantic lie?

"I get that." His gaze didn't leave her face. "I swear I'll do anything at all to find Brianna. To save her." He hesitated. "Or to protect you."

This new hurt joined the tumult of emotions in her chest. She closed her eyes for a moment, then said, "If we're going to eat, that's what we should be doing."

He only nodded and poured some nut and fruit mix into his hand, then tossed it into his mouth.

Mara was even less hungry now, but she crunched her way through enough to satisfy him, assuming he was paying attention, before dropping the small bag into an outside pocket of her pack.

As she hoisted her pack and herself to her feet, he didn't move, only watched her. Mara wasn't even sure he was breathing. But then he put his baggie of granola or whatever it was away and rose far more easily than she had.

"Why don't you take the lead now?"

How gracious of him. She wanted to hit him, to kick him. She also wanted his strong arms around her, so she could gather herself by soaking in that strength.

None of those options would make a single thing better. She'd have sworn she'd guarded herself against this kind of betrayal, but it turned out there were hidden weaknesses in the walls she'd built.

This was one of the reasons she refused to let herself really love anyone but her vulnerable niece. The little girl who was scared and waiting for her aunt to come for her.

Mara had to believe that.

*Chapter Eight*

Bri huddled with her back to a tree that grew at a sharp angle from the steep slope. She'd caught a glimpse a few minutes before of the stream or river or whatever it was that she was following. Just a shimmer, but that was enough to keep her from feeling completely lost. Now she crossed her arms over her knees and bent forward to rest her forehead on them. Eyes closed, she paid attention to her breathing, like that teacher in the stupid dance class had tried to teach them. Bri's effort didn't really work, partly because she'd hated everything about dance, especially the recital. Mom had insisted on it because she thought Bri was clumsy. But she wasn't. Her feet had grown before the rest of her, that was all.

The class was just one of the ways Mom had tried to fix her. All she'd succeeded in doing was convince Bri that she wasn't as pretty as her mom, as graceful, as smart.

Except if all of that was true, why had Mom ended up with such a creep? Not just one—there'd been a couple of other men before she met Dennis. Bri wondered about her dad, whom she didn't remember as well as she should. But she hadn't asked even her aunt Mara about him because she didn't want to know if he was another Dennis. What would that make her?

A trill from above startled her. It was followed by a funny little scratching sound really close to her. Heart pounding, she lifted her head slowly and saw a squirrel on a branch that she could almost touch. It was studying her with bright eyes, its fluffy tail jerking. He had something in his mouth.

Bri thought she might be smiling. She hadn't smiled since…she couldn't remember. Very softly, she said, "Hi."

The squirrel kept looking at her, as if she couldn't scare *him*. Only suddenly he swung to look somewhere past her, his movement faster than her eyes could see. The next second, he fled back to the trunk of his tree and raced up it to disappear.

Bri stayed frozen for longer than she should have. What if someone was scrambling up toward her? What if she wasn't as hidden as she thought she was?

*Look.*

She inched to take a peek. Nothing. It was so quiet. Too quiet, which made her realize she'd tuned out bird calls—but now even the smallest creature really had fallen silent. Was she breathing? She'd squirmed almost all the way around. Now she had to move just a little, so she could see past the rough trunk of the tree. Slowly. She couldn't make a sound.

A flash of white. That couldn't be part of the plane, could it? Hadn't she walked far enough to have left all of it behind? No, it was moving.

It was a man. He walked close to the creek, but his head kept swiveling. He was looking for something, and stepping really carefully, as if he was trying not to let his feet crunch on gravel or snap a stick underfoot or anything.

For an instant, she let herself feel hope. He could be one of the search and rescue people Aunt Mara had talked about. The trouble was, mostly she wouldn't recognize them. Only a couple of those people lived in Thunder Creek. Most had to come farther than that.

Only, why wasn't he wearing a pack? Or calling out her name?

Yes.

She had to stay hidden. Hide until she was *sure* anybody she saw was safe. Then she noticed something else her eye hadn't caught at first. The man carried a rifle, the kind some of the people in Thunder Creek used for hunting.

If he was hunting, Bri bet it wasn't for deer. She remembered the terrifying moments in the plane when she realized someone was shooting at them. The crumbling glass of the window, Mom screaming, Dennis… Bri wasn't sure. Swearing, maybe. She might have been screaming, too.

Search and rescue people wouldn't have any reason to carry guns, would they?

Hugging herself tight, Bri remembered that little black box she'd thrown in the river. Of course the bad guys would come looking. It had to be the money they wanted. The money Dennis must have stolen.

And if this guy was still looking for something, it was the duffel bag. Unless he hadn't found all the parts of the airplane yet, he'd have discovered that the shiny silver bag wasn't anywhere it should be. Not by one of the seats or in the cockpit with Mom and Dennis's mangled bodies or in the cargo area. And if he'd found *that*, he could probably tell that someone had opened all the bags and rifled through them. Bri had tossed things she didn't need on the ground, including those candy wrappers. This man would have known right away that someone had been there before him. Someone had either taken the bag with all that money or hidden it.

Bri inched back behind the tree so he wouldn't be able to see her. She tried to squeeze herself into the tiniest ball possible. She was as scared now as she'd been the moment when she knew the plane was going to crash.

What if Aunt Mara was looking for her, too? She'd have no way of knowing about the money or the gunshots that sent Dennis's plane down—or the man who might be willing to kill anyone who kept him from that money.

What if he killed the only person Bri had left in the world?

THE HELICOPTER PILOT contacted Cam's radio to let him know about the other searchers she'd dropped, and which directions they planned to hike. He didn't ask for the names of individuals, but he crossed his fingers that the coordinator had found more cops or law enforcement rangers.

Cam kicked himself for not laying down the law that all searchers had to be armed and trained to use the weapons. He'd give a lot to send Mara back to safety, along with the doctor and Walden, the mountain climber. Trouble was, he knew damn well that she'd refuse to go. Plus, the others were two of the most experienced search and rescue people around. Could he really send someone like Deputy Davis blundering off on his own?

Cam was temporarily in the lead, back to clambering over boulders. Mara had mostly kept her mouth shut since he'd told her why he had really appeared in Thunder Creek—and why he'd separated her from the crowd.

She was right; he'd planned their first encounters to be casual, seemingly natural. Thank God he hadn't kissed her the way he'd wanted to. There might have been no coming back from that. He'd seen right away that she had barbs like a hedgehog, that wariness was a big part of her personality. He doubted she forgave easily. *Focus on finding Bri*, he told himself. That's what mattered.

His mouth twisted. Sure. Mara would still be mad at him, and, face it, the odds were vastly against a fragile girl that age surviving a calamity like a plane going down in terrain as rough as any Cam had ever seen.

He swore under his breath. He had a job to do, one that had turned ugly, but this wasn't the first time in his career that had happened. Call it bad luck that a woman he liked, admired and wanted more than any he had in a long time was mixed up in this. And, okay, he hated the idea of seeing her hurt however it happened. He believed in his ability to protect Mara; Brianna was another matter.

The distant sound of a helicopter came to him from northeast of their current position. The pilot was keeping her promise to run a new grid as part of the search for the wreckage.

Around an hour later, Cam was still in the lead, swinging the machete again and cursing the black flies swirling around and biting, when a call came in on his radio.

He stopped, grateful to be able to let the machete drop to the ground. He took pride in his conditioning, but this was using muscles he'd apparently neglected. His right arm ached like a son-of-a—

His internal whining stopped once he had the radio in his hand. "Frasier here."

It was the pilot calling. Usually she sounded calm and professional. This time, what came out was a panicky jumble of words he had trouble distinguishing.

Mara, of course, had stopped, too, her anxiety visible.

"What happened?" Cam said into the radio. "I'm having trouble hearing you."

"Give me a second." Her breathing sounded as if she'd been running uphill. "I saw someone," she said finally. "A man waving a shirt. I thought he might be a survivor or a hiker or climber who'd seen something. I banked and flew toward him. He bent over. I thought he'd fallen down, but he was picking up a rifle. He…shot at me." She made an incoherent sound. "Not at—he shot *me*."

Cam had to stay calm, for his sake and hers. And for Mara's. "Did you make a crash landing?"

"No, I set the helicopter down on… I'm on the flank of Mount Crowder. He was on the ridge behind me, somewhere over, um, I think it must be Picket Creek."

Cam envisioned the map. "Pioneer Ridge, where you dropped us off?"

"Yes. That's it. I don't know how he got there, except he'd found a talus slope that allowed him to see any fly-overs." She'd hate to know how rattled she sounded. "I don't know how I kept on, but I don't think he can get to me here. My right arm isn't working, though. I don't dare—"

"Don't take any chances," he said sharply. "Dr. Cardoza and a deputy are heading straight toward you along Picket Creek. I'll call them, put them through to you so you can guide them."

He asked how many bullets she'd taken and where, how badly she was bleeding, and was somewhat reassured. She'd already grabbed an extra shirt and would keep putting pressure on her wound. Cam finished by asking if she'd seen what direction the shooter had gone but not surprisingly she hadn't. All that piece of slime had to do was step a few feet to be under tree cover. Cam did his best to close with encouragement, then immediately called Deputy Holmes, who carried the single radio assigned to that pair.

After hearing what Cam had to say, Lori handed the radio over to the doctor, who asked questions about the pilot's injury. He was brisk and confident and assured Cam that he and the deputy should be able to get to her with reasonable speed.

Which was probably still a minimum of a couple of hours, Cam thought grimly, depending on how high up on "the flank" she'd been able to land the helicopter.

Cam made the decision not to share the incident with Deputy Davis and Walden, even if he could reach them. They were too far away to help and should stay focused on trying not to miss any hint the plane had gone down in their vicinity. Ditto for the park rangers, although it was possible the pilot herself had contacted them.

The whole time he talked, Mara listened. Her eyes were huge, letting him see the shimmer of gold in the greenish brown. "I heard most of that."

He slapped at the swarm of insects as he summarized.

Her fingers had balled into fists. She seemed to be oblivious to the stinging flies. "Do you think he was trying to keep the helicopter from taking a path that would let the pilot see the crash site?"

"That's my guess. Which means it's either farther north than we estimated, up against Phantom Peak or Mount Fury—or it's south, probably the direction she was heading. And that means—"

"We're getting near it." She bounced on her toes as if she desperately wanted to sprint ahead.

Cam understood the impulse along with her single-mindedness, but he regretted even more that he'd allowed her to come. "We need to move farther away from the creek. We'll be harder to spot under the trees."

She opened her mouth as if to protest, quivered, then said, "It'll be even slower, but…you're right." She almost choked there at the end.

He rotated in place, searching the banks of the creek, the mess of alder and willow and spindly trees that might be maples threaded with ferns and a lot of plants he didn't recognize. No movement except the swirl of water wearing down boulders caught his eye. Anyone downstream of them wouldn't be able to see them, thanks to the jungle, but the hair on the back of his neck rose at the realization that the man who'd just shot a park ranger had been at a higher elevation than Cam and Mara—was he alone in being dropped out in this wilderness to head off rescuers? Cam had already been disturbed by the crackle underfoot when they had to step on the fallen brown leaves.

"Let's move uphill," he said, "then I want to take a look at the map again."

Mara followed without protest, her common sense suppressing what had to be intense agitation. Once he found a place sufficiently hidden in the trees, he knelt, swung his pack in front of him and dug out the map. He and she had been following Bald Eagle Creek, but he couldn't pinpoint how far they'd come. The forest and the low-valley jungle didn't vary. The map did show an unnamed creek that must be more of a waterfall than anything, and he'd neither seen it nor heard it.

Mara pointed out another waterfall, low at this time of year, that joined their creek but on the other side. That one, he'd noticed, as she obviously had. Unfortunately, they weren't far past it. He'd been thinking they should cross to the other bank that might be slightly more level, but studying the map, it didn't look good ahead. To his left, the land became steeper and steeper. They might need to rope up, which would slow them down even more, but they couldn't afford for one of them to fall. With it this steep, going straight up or down might be almost easier.

He debated.

Accustomed to making the decisions, he suspected that given her greater experience in these conditions, Mara would make better ones.

"What do you think?"

Surprised, Mara took a minute to wrench herself from the whirlpool of fear that wanted to suck her down. She wouldn't help Bri by doing something foolish that left her or Cam injured—or shot because they hadn't been cautious enough in their approach.

What popped out of her mouth was unexpected. "Why do you think they're out here searching, too?"

"Let's sit for a minute," he said. "This looks as close to flat as anyplace."

That must be why he'd picked it for them to stop. She nodded and carefully knelt before freeing herself of the bulky pack. Cam helped her get her arm through the strap before he laid down his rifle and shrugged out of his own pack.

"I think we can assume they know Terrell's plane went down and broke apart," he said, more matter-of-factly than she could be.

*Broke apart* was a picture Mara refused to let form in her head, but she agreed.

"Knowing the vicinity isn't the same as walking straight to it. In general, getting out here wouldn't have been any easier for them than it's been for us."

Also true, unless a helicopter had been able to unload men close to the crash site. The pilot had mentioned hearing another one. But Mara felt sure Cam had considered the same possibility.

"They may have needed to be sure Terrell is dead," he continued. "If he fled because he'd overheard something, seen something and was going to report them, they couldn't risk him surviving and, even if he was injured, making it to Ross Lake, say, or anywhere else that would have a ranger station or folks who could actually get a phone to work. I…went to his house to be sure he and Diana and Brianna weren't there. I saw a phone lying on the kitchen counter."

It was generally known that cell phone coverage was rarely possible within the park boundaries, which endangered people in the backcountry who couldn't call out for help after an injury. But who knew what Dennis had been thinking?

Mara bet Cam hadn't bothered waiting for a warrant before entering his suspect's house, but in this case she couldn't disapprove. Because he'd done that, they'd gotten going faster than they could have otherwise.

"If they left their phones, that suggests they didn't want to be traced. Which means—"

"He did something wrong," Cam said flatly.

The full horror of whatever decision Dennis had made hit her. No, not just Dennis; Diana must have agreed. "Would they really have just disappeared with Brianna?" she begged, as if Cam could tell her different.

He reached out and took her hand. She looked down at their clasped hands, seeing how his much larger hand engulfed hers in a way she hadn't noticed when he was just helping her over a rough spot. The strength of his grip let her take a mental step back from her panic and grief.

"Would Dennis be that much of a threat to people with so much money?" she asked. "I mean, as far as I know, he's a good pilot, but otherwise…"

"I agree." Cam didn't release her hand. "That's why I think he took something they need back. Pictures of incriminating evidence. A document, although I suspect they don't put a lot down on paper. So maybe someone went to the john and left a message or spreadsheet open and he got a screen shot. He could have even paged forward and then not remembered where he'd started, so whoever was working on whatever it was knew right away someone had seen it."

Mara winced. That sounded like something Dennis

would do. The only thing was… "I don't actually see him caring what his bosses are up to. Unless he thinks he can shake them down for a bigger share of the money, I guess. That's assuming he's a cog in their business and isn't just offering tourist flights."

"That's been my assessment of him." Cam sounded apologetic. He obviously didn't realize how much she disliked Dennis and even Diana. "My best guess is that he stole either drugs or money. If they're out for blood—and they'd have to be to go so far as to pursue his plane and force it down—that tells us he didn't take a shipment of cocaine that might have looked big to him but that they could shrug off. Ditto for money. He took a *huge* chance."

And unless he'd survived the crash and was rescued, he'd lost. Better to call it a suicidal chance. What Mara would never understand was how he could have risked Diana and Bri, too.

"That's…logical," she said, knowing she should pull her hand free and jump to her feet but not feeling ready. "They must know where the crash site is. Are they already there? It shouldn't take them long to grab their stolen property and disappear. If they're hanging around, *they're* the ones taking an enormous risk."

Speaking in a hard voice, he said, "Knowing the general area of the crash doesn't mean they could go straight to it. But, yes, going so far as to drop armed men to make sure they're not taken by surprise, they're taking a big risk. I have to wonder if they can't find whatever they're looking for."

Because they hadn't actually located the plane? Because the debris from the plane was scattered too far, shredded into unrecognizable pieces, some of it even inaccessible?

Or because they had reason to believe at least one of the three people on the plane had survived and helped him or herself to the stolen goods?

Right this minute, Mara's hope was at a low ebb. If anyone had miraculously survived a crash in these mountains, could they possibly be in any condition to hide from men hunting for them?

# *Chapter Nine*

The steep sidehill made the going even more difficult. Despite the support from his sturdy boots, Cam's ankles hurt and he felt as if they'd slowed to a crawl. He could only imagine how much their minimal progress chafed for Mara. They paused a couple of times so he could stay informed by the pilot, who could only wait, and the doctor and deputy trying to speed to her rescue.

He kept expecting Mara to show signs of the strain this cross-hill trek had on her, but if she felt any, she hid it. Was she truly so stoic, or was she so desperately fixated on getting to her niece, she wasn't aware of the beating her body was taking? With no makeup, brown hair pulled back into a tight knot, sweat gleaming on her forehead and a bruise he hadn't been aware of tinging a side of her jaw with purple, she was still beautiful in his eyes. He wished circumstances were different, that he could see her smile again.

If they didn't catch sight of the crash site in the not-too-distant future, they were going to have to spend another night out here. That would just about kill Mara, but days were getting short this far north in mid to late fall and were even shorter given that the sun disappeared behind mountains as high as Shuksan and Baker long before it sank over the ocean. How could he and she continue after dark?

They couldn't.

He'd become so accustomed to the occasional trills and calls from birds in the background along with darting movement of squirrels and chipmunks, Cam didn't register them anymore—until the sudden absence of any sound.

Mara, currently in the lead, didn't seem to have noticed. "I need to, um…" She waved toward a cluster of cedars crowding taller hemlocks uphill of them.

Already turning slowly to see what might have disturbed the wildlife, he nodded and said quietly, "Don't go far."

Her look would have pulled a smile from him at any other time. As it was, he continued to scan what he could of their surroundings with the eye of a man who'd fought halfway around the world in a country where death could come from a wreck of a car abandoned beside a road, a glint of light betraying a hidden sniper, what looked like a pile of dirty clothes. He'd feel better if he could identify what had triggered this new vigilance.

And then he heard a grunt and what might be a suppressed profanity. The profanity might be in his imagination; bears made grunts that could sound human. He cocked his head.

A voice snarled something he couldn't make out but was definitely human. It came from below, close to the creek and slightly behind where Cam and Mara had stopped.

He unsnapped his holster and his hand wrapped the butt of his gun. This had to be a stranger, maybe even the one who had shot the helicopter pilot. Although if so, how had he gotten here so fast?

A black uniform became quickly visible in the bright sunlight reaching the creek. Cam knew that uniform. He wasn't wearing it today but had been. Could that be Deputy Davis? If so...what was he doing here?

He was bounding from rock to rock, pushing off as he if wanted to sprint. Yeah, that was him, all right: uniform, tactical vest, dark green pack, hiking boots that didn't match the uniform. As the guy drew closer, Cam saw sweat dripping down his face and a distraught expression. Now what had gone wrong?

Cam stepped from behind his cover, a fir, and called, "Davis? That you?"

The deputy swung to spot him, stopped and bent forward with his hands on his knees, gasping for breath. "Thank God! Didn't know if I could catch you."

Somewhere behind Cam, Mara said softly, "Who is it?"

He flapped his hand behind his back and kept his voice low. "Stay out of sight."

"But—"

He gave his head a slight shake. Call him paranoid, but something about Reggie Davis had disturbed him from the beginning. He'd talked himself down, because presumably Bill Hayden knew the guy's background and had thought him a good choice for this search. Until Davis had pushed him about their assignments, Cam had mostly dismissed any instinctive unease. Sometimes you liked someone from first sight, sometimes you didn't. As far as he knew, Davis hadn't made anyone else in their group uncomfortable.

He raised his voice again. "What happened?"

Davis straightened, still breathing hard. "Shot. My partner. I dropped behind some rocks. They must have known where I was, because they started banging away. Walden had the radio. I couldn't get to him or call—" He breathed some more. "I knew where you were headed. Thought I could catch up. Better this way than to the others."

Davis, as the law enforcement half of that partnership, had started out carrying the radio. Should have continued carrying it. And as a cop, would he really have abandoned his partner whom he hadn't confirmed was dead?

Still, Cam waved him to climb toward him. "I'm thinking we might be close. We're trying to stay under cover."

"I might have blown that." The deputy stretched out a hand to push off a trunk as he started up toward Cam. "Sorry. Didn't think." His head turned. "Where's Mara?"

Cam spoke in a normal voice, knowing she'd be able to hear. He might feel like a fool in a minute, but better safe than sorry. "She hurt her knee about an hour ago. We agreed I had to go on. Glad you're here, since I'm increasingly suspecting the plane came down in this area."

Davis kept scrambling, looking genuinely like a man who'd traveled at his best speed. "We didn't see anything as far as we'd gone."

Cam leaned a shoulder against the rough bark of his sturdy support. "You couldn't have gone too far if you were able to catch up with me so soon."

"Farther than you'd think."

Trying to sound casual rather than sharply critical, he said, "If two men were up there lying in wait, didn't it occur to you that they didn't want you to continue up that creek for a reason?"

Davis bumped into another trunk of a forest giant and swore. He rubbed his shoulder with his right hand. Cam had noticed he was left-handed and tried to keep his eye on what that hand was doing. "Yeah, but I was reluctant to go on by myself. Thought if I could catch you soon enough, we could turn around."

"Did you?" Cam tried hard not to raise a skeptical eyebrow but wasn't sure he'd succeeded.

The deputy wasn't ten feet from Cam now. The two stared at each other. Out of the very corner of his eye, Cam saw a flicker of movement between trees up slope he could only hope Davis hadn't seen.

Mara was circling behind the man Cam deeply distrusted.

REGGIE WOULDN'T BE able to see her now unless he turned his head. Still, Mara flashed back to her National Guard deployment and her ability to move like a ghost. Good thing she'd already left the pack that would have hampered her before Cam lied to this volunteer. Given what she knew of his background, he probably didn't need backup, but she believed she'd read his signals right.

Funny—she'd been able to tell from the beginning that he didn't like Reggie. Normally, she'd have speculated more about why, because that wasn't like her. She met new volunteers in the local SAR group all the time. She'd have heard names and backgrounds, but even if she hadn't, she knew Bill didn't accept anyone off the street, and she trusted Bill. Her attitude had been to feel positive about the newcomers until they proved themselves incompetent or untrustworthy.

She had convinced herself she'd imagined any hint of resentment when Reggie looked at Cam—until it came out into the open. That was aggression she'd seen in his body language and the glitter in his eyes.

It appeared that Cam's instincts had been on target.

His posture not changing, he'd said something else that Mara hadn't heard. Didn't matter, since Cam's goal seemed to be trying to drag out the conversation.

She eased from tree to tree. Once her foot slipped, but she recovered without making a sound. The next tree trunk would put her directly behind Reggie. Already, his hefty pack blocked her view of his face and, mostly, of Cam.

"What's your problem?" Reggie snapped. "You think I should have charged on even if my partner was dead?"

"You sure Joe was dead?" Cam succeeded in sounding concerned.

Mara clenched her teeth. ·

"Didn't look good."

"Don't suppose the shooters would have let you go on, anyway." Cam paused. "You think of taking the two on? You're probably better trained with a firearm than they are."

"You mean, just gun them down? That's not what I do."

Mara might not be able to see Reggie's face, but she didn't miss the moment he pulled his handgun from his holster and held it slightly behind his thigh.

Cam...no, she couldn't tell exactly what *he* was doing, except he had to know where she was. Difficult as it was on a sideways pitch like this, she all but tiptoed forward, grateful for the moss cushioning her every step.

Reggie abruptly lifted his gun in both hands, aimed at Cam. She leaned to one side far enough to see that Cam had moved as fast. A standoff.

Mara pulled her own sidearm. Her thoughts spun. Shooting was a lousy option, given the bulk of the pack shielding Reggie's back, neck and even part of his head. Plus, if a bullet went through him—or she missed—she could hit Cam. *He* wouldn't want to shoot, either, for fear of hitting her. She took a slow breath. Firing wasn't smart anyway, because it would give away their presence to anyone within earshot.

The better choice was to use her own weapon as a blunt instrument.

*Yes.* Thank goodness she wasn't hampered by her own bulky pack.

"Work for the traffickers, do you?" Astonishing how conversational Cam could sound under the circumstances.

She felt sure he'd never once let his gaze stray past Davis.

"They pay better."

*Keep talking.* She took the last, short stride.

"Was this your plan from the beginning? Take care of whoever you got stuck with and then make sure nobody else made it to the crash site?"

"You could have avoided this if you'd listened to me."

Mara envisioned exactly how she'd have to move.

"But you still would have had to kill somebody."

*Me*, Mara thought in the corner of her mind not focused on what she had to do.

From the way the pack moved, Reggie had shrugged. "You're my first choice anyway."

"You're mine, too."

Time had run out. Mara slid her grip to the barrel of her Glock, leaped uphill to give her better reach…and swung as hard as she could. Davis started to turn, but not in time. The butt smashed into his head right behind the temple.

The force traveled up her arms, the sensation horrifying, but even as she readied herself for a second blow, she saw how his knees buckled. He staggered, hit the opposite side of his head on the rough bole of the closest tree, then went down as if he were a puppet, all the strings cut at the same time. Because of the sidehill, he half reeled around the tree and ended up facedown, skidding a few feet on the mossy hill.

Mara didn't move for a long time. Shaking, she was aware that Cam had swiveled to keep his weapon on this creep. With sudden and uncharacteristic savagery, she hoped Davis was dead.

Cam flicked a glance at her. "Good save." He only had to take a couple of steps to crouch to pick up Davis's handgun. For the moment, he tossed it aside, well away from the body. Still holding his own gun on the man, Cam eased downhill to where he could press his fingers to Davis's neck.

Mara hadn't moved. She made herself suck in air when she became aware she'd been holding her breath.

"He's dead," Cam said, standing. He kept his voice low as he holstered his gun and came straight to her. "Why don't you put that away?" he suggested gently, and she looked down to see that her own handgun hung dangerously at her side, barrel pointing upward at her.

She couldn't have labeled the sound that escaped her, but she did carefully turn the weapon and thrust it back into the holster.

His eyes never left hers. "Why didn't you tell me you were armed?"

"I…was going to, the next time we stopped."

"You know how to fire the thing, not just use it as a club?"

"Yes." The tremor in her voice told her what she'd done would stay with her, add to her nightmares. "I couldn't afford college, so I joined the national guard. It helped pay my way to a degree, although I had to do it slower than most of my friends." She paused. "I received thorough training and was deployed once, to Afghanistan. So this isn't the first time—" She couldn't say it.

"You've killed a man."

Her head bobbed.

"You're an extraordinary woman, even more so than I already knew." His expression tender, he reached out for her, and she flung herself into his arms.

If maybe a few tears slipped down her cheeks, she wiped them off on Cam's canvas shirt so he wouldn't see them. They came from her relief, she had to believe, not anything like grief…or horror.

SHE DIDN'T LET him hold her for long, which didn't surprise Cam, but he'd needed those couple of minutes and felt sure she did, too. He'd already admired this woman, who had shown him she would give her all for someone she loved. That was a quality more important to him than she could possibly know. He'd recognized her strength, too, but not guessed how innate a part of her personality it was.

Mara plopped down while he wrestled Reggie Davis's pack off his back and took time to inspect the contents. They weren't anything that would have given away his real intention; all Cam kept and added to his own pack was a spare magazine and the guy's wallet and, ironically, his badge.

And, yeah, the SAT radio. Which meant if Joe Walden was only injured, he had no way to call for help. Lucky Cam knew he could reach Dr. Cardoza and the deputy with him. The park rangers, who were closest to Walden, could turn around.

Rising, Cam looked down at the guy. Normally Cam would have felt bad leaving the body sprawled in the woods. He supposed eventually he'd send somebody back for whatever remained, but given the copious wildlife in this forest, there might not be much. His gaze flicked to Davis's left hand, and was glad to see no wedding band. Somebody might love him—a mother, a girlfriend—but this man would have murdered Cam and Mara in cold blood with no hesitation.

Joe was another matter. Cam got on his radio and received an immediate response.

"Hallquist here." One of the rangers was Brent Hallquist. "Find something?"

"No." Still speaking quietly, Cam explained what had happened as well as his assumption that the crash site lay ahead of his and Mara's route. He asked that Hallquist and his partner go to Joe Walden's aid.

Hallquist did some swearing before promising him

they'd move as quickly as possible. They had been close to the headwaters of Mineral Creek anyway. They knew that the pilot had been shot and were therefore aware that even that far north, they could be in danger.

"Don't know if we'll make it before dark, but we'll do our best."

"Stay in touch," Cam said.

"Count on it."

Stowing the radio in an outside pocket of his pack, Cam told Mara, "You'd better go grab yours. Let's keep moving. We don't have long until dark." An hour, at a guess. Not enough. Not for them and not for Joe Walden.

She complied, and once Mara joined him with her pack, Cam set out in the lead. He didn't spare a glance back and doubted Mara did, either.

Dusk had arrived when he held up his hand to stop her again. This time, a couple of crashing sounds heralded the distant appearance of a man between tree trunks, albeit closer to the creek than they were. His denim shirt didn't blend well with a northwest forest, and neither did the white T-shirt he wore beneath. The semiautomatic rifle he carried slung over his shoulder was an obscenity in this environment, given his purpose.

Damn, Cam wished he had a sniper's rifle fitted with a suppressor. His conscience didn't even ping at the thought.

Initially the guy progressed toward them, but even from a distance his scowl was visible. Finally he swore loudly enough that Cam heard him and turned to go back the way he'd come. Once he stopped long enough to stab the barrel of the rifle into what, from a distance, appeared to be the fern-filled well around a forest giant.

Apparently finding nothing, he kicked a nearby nurse log. Rotting wood flew, and he hopped a couple of times.

Served him right.

Cam gestured to Mara, and they both crouched, watching and waiting until he was out of sight.

"He wasn't trying to be quiet." An agony he understood infused her voice.

The likeliest explanation was that everyone in the wreckage was dead. However many men who'd made it out here were searching for the missing something, not some*one*. But Cam wasn't ready to give up hope.

"He must have figured nobody could have made it any farther or he'd have seen them."

"Well, he was wrong, wasn't he?" Mara's shadowed gaze hadn't strayed from where the guy had disappeared.

Did he know that the turncoat Deputy Davis had been hustling this way to stop Cam and Mara? Nothing suggested he did. This was like fighting a guerrilla war, with no idea how many troops the enemy had fielded.

The really big question Cam had to ask himself, was how far this particular man had come from the crash site. How close were they? Did he and Mara dare risk sneaking forward even as the purple of the sky deepened?

Cam realized how dim their surroundings had become. "We have to stop for the night," he said regretfully.

Her gaze swung to his. "We can't! Not now!"

He touched her lips with his fingertips. "Hush. Let's not make his mistake."

That had to be a whimper from her, and he understood completely. Quitting so close to their goal didn't make him any happier than it did her, even if he didn't feel the same terror for a child he loved.

He'd seen the kid, though, seen the way Mara looked at her. The last hug. Yeah, for Mara, he'd do almost anything—but either Brianna was dead, hiding or under guard. Advancing now would be foolish, and that was something they couldn't afford to be. Two against…who knew how many?

# *Chapter Ten*

Bri had seen two different men pass so close, she could have asked for help in a normal voice, no shouting required. Both of them carried rifles, which scared her to death. She huddled behind a tree each time, not making a sound. Not even breathing, because who knew how far away someone could hear even that tiny giveaway?

She couldn't see the creek anymore, but ages ago she'd realized seeing it wasn't necessary. *Duh*, she'd thought. No matter how high she climbed, all she had to do was go downhill to find herself within sight of the water. She kind of missed it, though. It made a musical, burbling sound that reminded her of Mrs. Marshall's newborn baby when he pursed his lips and blew out. Even the glimmer of sunshine off the water was welcome. But she was safer up here, lost amid all these giant trees.

Every so often she tipped her head back and tried to see the tops but couldn't. She could hear a *shush* occasionally that might be a breeze up at the top of what Aunt Mara called "the canopy."

Thinking about Aunt Mara hurt. It was like Bri's heart turned into a knot and forgot it was supposed to beat. She saw her face, and the way she smiled, sort of…merry. Bri didn't even know where that word came from, just that

Aunt Mara's smile wasn't like anyone else's. Bri loved her aunt's touch, too, the gentle way she'd stroke Bri's hair back from her face, studying her with a softness that said *she* thought Bri was pretty.

She couldn't let herself remember Mom's face. All that came was the one, horrific sight. She wanted to forget but had a really awful feeling she would never be able to.

She'd walked farther—maybe for as long as an hour—after seeing the last man, but in sudden alarm she discovered she could hardly see her feet. Or even her hand, when she held one up in front of her. She should probably stop—

With her last step, there was nothing for her foot to come down on. She crashed forward, reaching out. She hit the humungous tree so hard, Bri heard a bone snap. Then she fell into a hole. Something rustled all around her and scraped her bare face. She landed on her side, and it was as if night had fallen between one second and the next.

What terrified her most was that she might have screamed.

She swallowed a whimper. She had already hurt, so much, but now her arm and elbow screamed in comparison. Hot tears rolled down her face as she lay unmoving, trying to understand what had just happened. It was like somebody had set a trap...except she suddenly knew. This was one of those holes that surrounded some of the trees. It was the same as the one where she'd hidden the duffel bag, except this one was filled with ferns. She'd seen ones like this a lot today without realizing how deep the holes went.

Bri cradled her arm close to her body. Would she even

be able to get *out* of this hole with only one usable hand and arm? Then, panicking, she thrashed around in search of her duffel bag. The one that held her only food and the blanket and parka she'd squeezed inside.

The strap wasn't around her shoulder, the way it had been. She couldn't have dropped the duffel before she fell, so it *had* to be in here with her. It just had to be.

When her hand found something rounded and squishy, she cried even harder. At least tonight she wouldn't freeze. Tomorrow was soon enough to try to figure out how to escape the trap she'd blundered into.

As much as she hurt, she didn't even care that she was thirsty and the stream was so far away.

Why hadn't Aunt Mara found her yet?

CAM CALCULATED HOW best to lay out their tarp and sleeping bags to allow him to see *anyone*—or thing—approaching Mara and him once they were tucked up for sleep. She didn't contribute to his debate, probably agreeing with his belief that the man they'd seen wouldn't be coming back this way in the near future, especially in the dead of night.

He winced at his thoughts and was glad he hadn't spoken them aloud.

He chose a semi-level piece of ground above the trunks of two trees that must have grown from small shoots together. Unless Mara planned to go find her own tree, they just about had to nestle together.

Both lowered their packs to the ground. Cam used his booted foot to scrape the space a little flatter, then stifled a groan as he lowered himself, too. Either Mara was still more limber than he was, or she was a champ at hiding whatever she felt. If that was so, what had happened to teach her such a harsh lesson?

"Do you think Lori and Dr. Cardoza have gotten to the pilot yet?" she asked quietly.

"Probably not." He frowned at the darkness. "I'd sure like to know about Walden, too, but I'm thinking I need to keep the radio silenced."

"Oh." It was barely an exhalation. Then, "Yes! Except… that isolates all of us."

It did. Cam wasn't comfortable doing that, but the way his skin was prickling, he believed he and Mara were dangerously close to the crash site and the ruthless men searching the vicinity. Under other circumstances, he'd have been tempted to try to make a silent approach to get an idea what they faced—and whether they'd set up camp right beside the torn remnants of the sleek little Beechcraft plane.

Had they lit a fire to warm themselves and hold back the night? Were they bothered by any corpses trapped in the torn metal or flung aside? Cam doubted it. The kind of people who signed on to work for drug traffickers weren't what you'd call empathetic. Amoral and narcissistic were better descriptions.

He hated knowing that tomorrow he'd be risking this woman's life. Not that he'd say that to her. After all, she'd saved *him* only a couple of hours ago.

Once he started digging in his pack, she did the same. They agreed they could set up a camp stove and cook a meal. Hers—homemade—looked better than his, and they agreed on a curried chicken to be followed with candy bars.

It actually smelled good, to his mild surprise, and

tasted better. They should have made more stops to eat today, he realized. Going short on food in favor of speed hadn't been smart.

Talking quietly felt safe. He asked, "Is Bri's dad alive?"

He sensed her stillness. "My brother? No. He died in a drunk driving accident. A tragedy, right? Except he was the drunk, and he killed someone else in the car he hit head on as well as himself."

He set down his dish and reached out to squeeze her hand. "I'm sorry. That's tough."

"My father was an alcoholic, too." Even as soft as her voice was, the wryness came through. "He died from cirrhosis of the liver. I'd happily carry a banner for prohibition."

"Don't blame you."

She squeezed his hand in return, then reclaimed hers. "You don't seem to drink much."

"I don't like to feel out of control. A beer is okay. Much more than that…" He shrugged. "You'd think your, er, sister-in-law would have been more careful about the next man in her life."

"She never seemed to mind, but that's probably because she likes her booze, too. You may have noticed that she and Dennis spent a lot of time at the tavern."

He had, because from the minute he became involved in this investigation, he'd locked on to the pilot who he'd concluded had to be working for the group building the resort. Why else had Terrell moved his operation to a backwater town like Thunder Creek the minute that airstrip had gone in? The town boasted exactly one bed and breakfast, so tourists weren't waiting in line to book a bird's eye view of the sites, however spectacular the views would be.

Sounding hesitant, Mara asked about his family. He talked about what was probably a pretty typical upbringing for a kid with middle-class parents. He told her that he and his dad had butted heads for as long as he could remember, but that his father had been a steady man. He would do anything for any member of his family.

He waited for her to pull her pad and sleeping bag out of her pack to signal that personal confidences were at an end, but she surprised him.

"Are you married?"

That she was curious, he liked, but the question itself offended him. "You think I'd have asked you out if I was married?"

"It was for your job. It's not like we did anything you'd have to apologize to your wife for."

"I'm divorced," he said shortly. "No kids, thank God."

"You don't want any?"

"I do, but not with Joanne." Aside from tersely telling his parents and brother what had ended his marriage, he hadn't talked about it. Not even with his closest friends. Why would he want anyone to know that his wife had cheated on him because she hated his long absences while he was gaining a foothold in the FBI?

Assuming that was her only reason. He'd spent too much time wondering if the dispassion his job demanded of him had made him distant, cold. Would he have recognized that?

She'd never said anything like that, though, only whining every time he packed for an investigation or called to let her know he wouldn't make it home until late or the next day.

Whatever her reasons, the trust marriage required was like a precious piece of glass that slipped from your hands. No, worse—it was glass his wife had flung at the wall and not cared when it shattered into sharp, broken pieces.

Since then, he'd been involved with a few women but never with an eye to the future. Certainly not to the point where he'd talk about his past.

So why was he considering doing just that now? Where was this odd sense of intimacy coming from? His instant attraction to this woman?

The answer was easy. It was because anyone Mara loved would be able to trust her. He'd known her a matter of days, but her unflinching determination to find her niece had told him she'd never let down a man she loved, either.

She'd been peripheral in his original research. Just a way to get close to Dennis Terrell. She'd been right; he had used her. That made him wince. Was it something they could get past?

He hadn't specifically found a marriage in her history and figured she'd implicitly give him permission to ask in turn, "You?"

"No," she said softly. "Once I thought—" She shook her head. "It doesn't matter."

"Sure it does."

"We should get some sleep."

Pushing didn't seem like a good idea, so he agreed. Five minutes later, they'd laid out their bedding and taken turns going behind a nearby tree to take care of their needs.

He unlaced his boots, as she did, and pulled off his shirt. Mara seemed to hesitate before she removed her own top layer to reveal what he could tell was a short-sleeve T-shirt only because her arms gleamed in the faint light. She seemed to agree with his decision not to strip any further in case of a need to move fast.

He wadded up his parka to serve as a pillow and felt her wriggle as she did something similar. Too warm to be completely enclosed in his sleeping bag, he clasped his hands under his head. Then they lay in silence, both on their backs staring upward. Cam gradually relaxed, his body happy to quit for the day, but his mind not close to ready to shut down. Mara was too still, even rigid, to be any readier.

"I was really set on being an FBI agent," he heard himself say. He didn't believe anyone more than a couple of feet away would be able to hear him. "The better job you do, the more that's asked of you. I thought my wife understood that, knew that eventually I'd be promoted to more of a desk job or at least be able to pick and choose."

"But she didn't," Mara whispered. "Oh, Cam." She rolled onto her side to face him.

"She had a job she seemed to like. Friends. It wasn't as if I'd dragged her along on a transfer to a new city."

"Which would have happened eventually."

"I'd warned her about that, too, but it hadn't happened yet." He wished he could see Mara's face. "I surprised her in bed with another man. I turned to walk out, and she screamed at me." He'd kept going, sick but probably keeping his shock from his face. He was good at hiding emotion behind an imperturbable facade.

That led him back to wondering if she'd seen too much of that impassive facade, never understanding who he was behind it.

Mara's hand settled on his chest . From most women, he'd expect words of sympathy, gushing reassurance. Instead, Mara's hand moved, circling, patting him. Reassurance enough. His muscles released some of the tension.

"The next morning, she called to tell me she hadn't known how hard marriage to me would be." He surprised himself by continuing. "At least before we got together she'd had a roommate. If I'd really loved her, I'd have quit my job once I could tell she hated it. This was *my* fault."

Mara snorted.

Cam felt a grin pull at his mouth. Now, this was a woman who might miss her husband, feel lonely, but would scoff at the idea of long absences being "too hard." What's more, if he'd seemed withdrawn, she'd have gotten in his face and demanded an explanation.

Her soft voice came from the darkness close by. He imagined he could feel the warmth of her breath. "It's lucky you didn't have children."

"Yeah." At least both of them had been able to walk away, not be tied for a lifetime.

Would Mara feel an exchange of confidences was only fair? Cam hoped so.

She didn't disappoint him. "Turns out you and I have something in common," she said wryly. "During the year my national guard unit was deployed, I fell for a guy from another unit. We spent any spare time together. We talked about the future. I think that was the worst part. Why would he take the pretense that far? Meantime, he stayed in close touch with a woman he said was his sister."

"He was *married*?"

"Yep." Mara made a little sound. "We'd decided we were going to have two children. It would be nice if we had a girl and a boy, but it didn't really matter. We even talked about where we wanted to live."

He lowered his arms so he could wrap one around her, however awkward the position. "What a dirtbag."

"I've thought worse, but that sums him up pretty well. Only... I felt stupid. Given the mess my family had been and my brother's problems, how could I not spot the lies?"

"It wasn't your fault. You know better than that. This was all on him. He was a con man, well-practiced." Cam gently tugged, until she scooted close enough to put her head on his shoulder. "Two of a kind," he muttered.

"Two of—? Oh. Your wife and my husband-to-be." She was quiet long enough, he thought she'd said everything. But then she gave a half laugh. "I wondered whether Jason would feel a twinge of conscience, say, when his wife threw herself into his arms at the airport. But then another guy from his unit told me he'd had a girlfriend on his previous deployment, too."

"Too damn hard being on his own for a stretch." His choice of words was deliberate. "And you should have punched the other guy for keeping his mouth shut for so long."

Mara muffled what had to be a laugh against his chest. He smiled and tightened his hold on her.

An owl hooted overhead. He could feel Mara's breath

now, with his throat bared. He wanted to kiss her like he couldn't remember wanting anything in a long time but knew that would be a mistake. Sleep beckoned, but he wasn't ready to cut off this quiet talk. "Tell me about Brianna."

"Oh. When she was born, she looked so mad."

Cam loved the soft laugh.

"I fell in love with her. I knew how unstable my brother was, and I'd never liked Diana. I swore that no matter what happened with them, Bri would have me. So... I probably made things worse by babysitting anytime they'd let me, involving myself in Bri's life." Pause. "Moving to stay close to her."

"Why do you say 'worse'?" he asked.

"Maybe if I hadn't been so eager to take up the slack, they'd have done better to face up to their responsibility."

"Do you think that's how it works?"

Her fingers curled around his sleeping bag. "No. But the truth is, Bri is fine. She's good-hearted, loves animals, is way ahead of grade level in school. I don't actually think she lacks anything."

Present tense. Cam didn't know if he could hold on to that much hope.

But then Mara whispered, "I'm scared."

"I know." Cam shifted a little to settle her closer to the length of his body. "I wish I could promise you—"

"That would make it worse."

Worse? Oh. Him making a promise he'd always known he wouldn't be able to keep. That would strike home for her.

He murmured, "Good night," and behind his closed eyelids pictured Brianna Dawson's face with those big eyes, a pointy chin and ears that stuck out more than she'd probably like. A pixie, he thought now, who was taking after her aunt.

If that was so, the girl might be as gutsy as the woman, as determined not to give up.

He hoped she had a chance. His sinuses burned. He'd do just about anything to find Brianna alive and well, for Mara's sake.

# Chapter Eleven

Clutching the duffel with her good arm, Bri held herself in a tight, trembling ball. Her teeth chattered. She hurt so much, she didn't even try to fumble with the zipper to pull out the blanket, and she wasn't hungry. Only thirsty, but her bottle was empty. Even if it held plenty of water, how could she twist the top off with one hand?

*Hold it between your knees*, some practical voice in her head said. But that would mean moving, and she didn't have water anyway because she hadn't planned well enough to refill the bottle.

If only Aunt Mara were here.

*Where are you?* she wailed silently. But she also knew how foolish she was being. How could anyone find her in this dense forest of giant trees? Aunt Mara could pass five feet from her and not see her—or the other way around.

As the night crept on, Bri wished passionately that she hadn't taken that money and hid it. She'd hated and wanted revenge, but if she'd left it lying where it was, the bad people probably would have grabbed it and left. Why would they even have looked for her? She could be sitting now by the tail of the plane—*not* the nose—and waiting for rescuers.

In her pain, hating Dennis, too, was easy, and even her mom, who should have known better.

The darkness gave Bri a different kind of shiver. What if she was already dead? Was this what it would be like? Only pitch-black with no glitter of starlight? Complete aloneness? No sensation, no—

Well, then, she couldn't be dead, could she? Because while her pain had lessened into near numbness, it was there, a sharp kind of warning. If she moved at all, she'd be sorry.

As cold as she was, as hungry, she *had* to move.

MARA WASN'T SURPRISED that her sleep was so restless; the slope that kept rolling her into the man beside her wasn't exactly comfortable. The way she kept waking up to find their bodies as enmeshed as the sleeping bags would allow, his arm wrapped securely around her, *was* comfortable, and troubling.

She tried opening space between them or lying on her other side, knees pulled up to her stomach, but no. Next time she'd awaken, there she was again. The night felt endless. She couldn't possibly be sleeping for more than forty-five minutes or an hour at a time.

When her eyes opened to the crisp dark silhouette of branches above her against a pale gray sky, she was incredibly grateful.

Grateful…and terrified. It seemed almost certain that this was the day she'd find out whether Brianna had miraculously survived—or whether she was dead.

The man beside her stirred. His arm tightened, too, which made her realize that, yes, she was once again lying pressed to his longer body, her head on his shoulder instead of the soft ball of her parka.

She held herself very still, even as she wanted desperately for them to leap up and *go*, now that they were so close. If he sank back into sleep for even another few minutes, though, she could inch away so he didn't know they'd spent the night cuddling.

But, of course, he made a growly sound and turned his head. Their eyes met, his close to the color of the dawn sky.

"I'm sorry if I woke you," she said stiffly.

"No." He cleared his throat. "I'm glad these tree trunks are so broad. Otherwise, we'd have probably woken up in the creek."

She tried for a smile that, from his expression, must not have been very convincing. Then she squirmed until she could sit up. Already the sky had lightened. Glad she was still mostly dressed, she unzipped her bag and scooted out. Boots on, she scrambled toward the next closest tree that would give her a moment of privacy.

When she returned, Cam had already either done the same or not progressed that far. He'd put on a fleece quarter-zip and was poking in his pack.

"Granola?" he asked.

"That sounds fine." Except she wasn't really hungry. "Unless we crunch too loudly."

One side of his mouth tipped up. "Nobody is that close to us."

His jaw was covered by distinct bristles. Every line on his face had seemingly deepened in the past twenty-four hours. A couple of scratches had oozed tiny drops of blood that had dried in place. His dark hair, unruly at best, looked as if he'd just scrubbed his hands through it.

She didn't even want to think about what her hair was doing, except she'd be more comfortable if she could dig her brush out of her pack and find an elastic. First, though, she struggled into her denim shirt, then her parka. She was more conscious this morning of how chilly the air was. A first snowfall wasn't far away in these rugged mountains.

He set out the open bag of granola, but she brushed her hair first and fastened it back, then winced as she felt scratches on her face, too. She tried to be surreptitious when she swallowed a couple of ibuprofen with water, as if she'd be admitting to weakness.

Finally, she took a handful of the granola. "Do we have a plan?"

"We?"

She scrunched up her face and was immediately sorry. "You."

He paused just as he'd been about to toss granola in his mouth. "I wish I did."

They both chewed and swallowed. Even as her body ached, Mara's nerves buzzed. They shouldn't be taking their time. They had to *hurry*.

As if he'd read her mind, he said, "We need to talk before we do anything else."

He was right, which didn't prevent any delay from being agonizing.

"Why haven't you called for help?" she asked. "I mean, it's just the two of us, and we know we're getting close. Could the park service send another helicopter?"

The furrows in his forehead deepened more. "These

scumbags have successfully grounded one. What I wish I knew is how many people they have out here, and how well armed they are. What if they have something like an RPG?"

A rifle-propelled grenade. She'd seen one bring down a helicopter. The memory was one of her worst from her year of service.

"Why would they?" she argued. "I mean, how could they predict whatever problem has them beating the bush?"

"They're probably not quite that well-armed—you're right, they're facing something unexpected and seem to be running around in circles—but we know they do have automatic and semiautomatic weapons."

Yes, she'd seen those, too.

"Which are almost as good. Helicopters are so damn noisy, anyone who wanted to shoot it down would have plenty of time to set up."

His rifle was a semiautomatic, too, but compared to their opponents, the two of them were poorly armed. She'd felt good because she had a handgun, but this was more like guerrilla warfare than facing off with one or two traffickers.

"I started with some misconceptions," he said bluntly. "I don't make mistakes often, but in this case… Hell, I have something in common with them. I don't know how I could have foreseen this fiasco."

A bird chattered right above as if commenting. It flew away before Mara could focus on it. "Misconceptions?"

"I called out search and rescue because that seemed most logical." He grimaced. "Our priority. Yes, I knew the plane had been forced down, but let's face it, small plane crashes are almost invariably fatal to anybody on board."

She flinched.

"I'm sorry."

"I understand."

"I anticipated they might send another small plane or a helicopter to confirm that Terrell's Beechcraft had indeed crashed. That's why I wanted most searchers to be armed, just in case one of us stumbled on an armed man who had the same goal of finding the plane. But what's going on here is nothing I expected."

"They're willing to do anything to stop us from locating the crash site."

"Yeah. At first, I assumed the goal was being sure Terrell was dead, in case he'd stolen some information or had the idea of making a deal with the feds. You know that. But now, I think they must have found the plane. So why haven't they hustled back to their everyday jobs rather than risk getting caught out here in a national park shooting at rangers?" He grunted. "Just getting caught carrying outlawed weapons without special permission would guarantee them a hard slap from a federal judge."

"Do you think Dennis did survive?" she asked tentatively. "And somehow got away?"

"That's one possibility." Cam shook his head. "He almost had to be injured and rattled. Going on the run, sure, but does he have any background in the wilderness? Hiking, hunting…?"

"No. That's one reason I was shocked when Diana announced they were moving up here. A tiny town at the edge of civilization? An hour and a half drive to the closest mall?" Okay, that might be an exaggeration but not much of one. "Neither of them were interested in hiking, climbing, cross-country skiing. It seemed so unlikely a choice, but Dennis was really pumped about the offer to be the principal pilot for a high-end resort."

"Putting in the runway and hangars makes sense to attract wealthy vacationers who like to fly to their destination. Otherwise…why would the resort need a pilot? Sure, it's great that they can offer scenic flights, but he was already doing that. Most supplies will still need to come in by truck."

"I know." She pressed her lips together. "I *like* hiking and all the rest. But I moved because…" She could only be honest, as she believed he had been. "Because Diana quitting a well-paying job, them taking Bri out of school where she thrived, just didn't make sense."

"No." Was that pity in his eyes? Or just compassion? "That's why I focused on Terrell right away."

It stung, remembering that he'd focused on her right away for the same reason. But hurt feelings were barely a blip on her current radar. Only Bri mattered. "Okay."

"If I'd been able to arrow in more closely on where the plane went down, I wouldn't have divided our group the way I did. I'd be glad to have the park rangers with us, for example. But finding out a deputy was dirty, and then losing our other deputy and the doctor because the pilot was shot…" He shook his head. "Probably thanks to Davis, *they* knew where to place their pawns. We're blind. They had eyes on us from the beginning."

"But…can't you, well, call in reinforcements? Something like the FBI Hostage Rescue Team?"

"Reinforcements, yes. The HRT? No. They're more focused on counterterrorism, not a possible death or two during an investigation into an organization linked to smuggling cartels. We have regional tactical teams, though. In fact, I do have one on standby. But I have the same problem I started with. We haven't yet definitively located any debris from the crash, and we don't know if there are survivors."

"If there are..."

"Once too many bullets start flying, they wouldn't have a chance."

Cam would be shocked if there were any survivors, but he understood why Mara wanted so desperately to believe that Bri had defied the odds. If the traffickers were searching only for something Terrell had stolen, though, why couldn't they find it? Yeah, the debris would certainly be far-flung, but to take *days* for the hunt? Unless they were frantically searching for something small— say, a laptop or phone—why would it be more than a few hundred yards from the crash site?

The plane could have crumpled, he supposed. Separating a ball of twisted metal would be a job, and a noisy one even if they'd thought to bring in some suitable tools. Cam had no doubt he and Mara were near enough now, they'd have heard anything like that.

If Diana or Bri had survived, why go to such extremes to find them before SAR could? Was it even remotely possible that either of them knew anything irrefutable? As an explanation, that didn't satisfy him, either.

In fact, asking himself endless questions wasn't helping. He had to set eyes on the crash site, get a good idea how many men surrounded it and what they were doing before he dared summon a tactical team. Which meant moving but even more slowly, more cautiously. He couldn't help wishing again that he could tuck Mara somewhere safe while he made the approach, but she'd blast him if he suggested any such thing, and doing so didn't make sense anyway. She moved more naturally in this wilderness than he did, had sharp eyes, combat experience... and had already proven her ability and willingness to provide backup.

He just preferred to think of Mara safe at home. And that was because he'd been stumbling into...not quite love, not this fast, but he'd felt something powerful from the beginning.

*Live with it*, he told himself, hardening his heart. As it turned out, she was probably the best backup he could have had from the whole bunch. So far, he hadn't needed a doctor or a climber. He'd needed a fellow soldier. He just wished she were less emotionally invested. Could she keep quiet if she saw her niece, for example?

Cam shook off the thought. Again...what were the chances of that?

"All right," he said. "Stay within sight of me if you can. Hand signals only."

She nodded, stuffed the few things she'd gotten out of her pack back in it and rose to her feet. She holstered the handgun—a Glock, he thought—last. He glanced down at his watch. Today, he'd stay more aware of the time.

The woods were eerily quiet as they moved. He'd expect more chirping with daylight, but maybe the presence of the two humans was silencing the birds. One faint rustle had him turning sharply, but all he saw was a lowslung cedar branch shaking. Mara didn't make a sound.

Perhaps an hour into their slow, difficult progress

across the steep sidehill, his nostrils flared. That smelled like…bacon? *Please don't let these idiots have built a fire.* There'd be no faster way for all of them to die than to lose control of even a few hot cinders from a campfire. The smell didn't grow any stronger, though, and he decided they might be cooking some freeze-dried breakfast. He paused, evaluating what breeze there was. Had to be wafting toward Mara and him, which was fortunate.

Sure enough, a little later he heard voices. Not loud, not urgent, but at least two people talking. Cam glanced over his shoulder and raised his eyebrows. Mara nodded; yes, she'd heard, too. New tension showed on her face.

He eased from one enormous tree trunk to the next, head cocked as if that would help him hear better.

Slow. Quiet. The green light made him feel as if he were under the sea.

He made out words. "If we haven't—"

*Haven't what?*

Should he and Mara gain a little more elevation? He could just faintly hear the creek. Of course, no reason to think the Beechcraft had descended directly into the creek or onto its bank. Terrell would have lost control of his plane during the descent.

Cam wished again that he had a suppressor on his handgun. Coming face-to-face with one of these bastards would be a disaster. Damn, what if Davis had somehow gotten word to his compatriots to expect two rescuers? They might even know he was a fed.

If so, wouldn't they have folded up their operation? Or did they have no problem with the idea of killing a few more people?

Of course they didn't. However they'd accomplished

the feat, they'd likely been close enough to see terror on the faces of the people in the airplane they'd driven into the ground. Battling opponents abroad, he'd always known men who wanted to kill him at least fought fiercely for their own principles, their homelands, their families. Despicable though some of those principles might be through his lens, those men had a leg up on drug traffickers with no principles at all. Had they felt anything when they found the wreckage and likely the bodies?

*Knock it off*, he told himself. *Don't screw up because you're brooding.*

Another glance back. For a moment, he didn't see Mara at all, and he froze. Then she appeared from behind a big fir or hemlock just uphill from him. Of course she hadn't vanished. What was wrong with him? He couldn't afford divided attention.

It was essential to know at all times where his partner was.

His eyes met hers, and for a little too long, neither of them moved.

"Where could she be?" a louder voice demanded.

Mara's eyes widened.

Cam couldn't make out the mumbled response. He didn't let himself jump to the conclusion that the *she* in question was either Bri or Diana. There could well be women involved with this group. He knew damn well that Mara hoped that *she* was Brianna. No surprise when she'd been holding on to that hope all along.

*God, let her be right.*

But nothing had changed. The goal was the same. He needed to see the pieces of wreckage and any bodies.

How many of these scumbags were here? Why had they been here for days?

Raking the slices of faintly lighter openings between trunks with his gaze, Cam eased forward. With each step, he paused, listened, searched his surroundings. Checked on his partner.

Her tension felt like a taut string between them, a familiar sensation to him from dangerous moments when he depended on someone he knew well. There'd been occasions over the years when he'd have sworn the connection was two-way, that they *were* communicating.

Scraping rough bark with his shoulder, he eased around yet another tree. A blotch of white appeared, unnatural in this green and gray landscape.

He stepped a little farther and realized he had to be seeing the nose of the plane. It was contorted and compressed between two trunks. There were no wings, no cabin, no tail—but this was unquestionably the missing plane. The windshield was shattered.

He lifted a hand and signaled for Mara, who slipped silently to his side. Her eyes widened again, her lips parted, and he put his hand over her mouth even though he didn't really think she'd gasp out loud.

She was breathing hard, though, and he knew she saw what he did: two dead people in that cockpit.

# Chapter Twelve

The voices gained in volume. No, Mara just picked out what was being said better. Mumbles interspersed with curses and what sounded like a few curt orders.

Cam moved ahead of her like the soldier he'd been, lightly balanced on the balls of his feet despite the increasingly steep, moss-covered side of the creek valley shaped more like a V than a U. He might have been a cat, picking its way toward prey that had no idea of the danger.

Even scared, she did her very best to match him. Her ankles ached fiercely from walking on the sidehill for so long. But, oh God, they'd found what remained of Dennis's airplane. It had begun to feel illusive, as if she might never know what had become of it. Seeing the hideous sight of the cockpit with what had to be two heads covered with flies or some other kind of insect, had made this real. The force required to tear the plane into pieces like this was nearly unimaginable to her.

No, she didn't want to imagine it, because then—

He abruptly lifted a hand to signal a stop. Beyond him, she saw movement. Men in a sort of circle. She couldn't tell how many were bunched together, but it had to be half a dozen of them. Some were crouched. They were arguing loudly. These were clearly not the leaders. They wanted to go home. They were beginning to resent the orders that had them scrambling up and down what looked like a mountainside, or over and around boulders. One grumbled that his wet boot hadn't dried out overnight at all. If they could light a fire—

"Don't be an idiot!" someone snapped. "We could burn this forest down."

"Who cares?" another man mumbled.

"Don't call *me* an idiot!" snarled one who had been kneeling but now leaped to his feet. Even from this distance, he bristled with aggression.

*That's it. Get in a fight.* Mara remembered Cam asking if she'd ever seen a brawl and she'd had to say no. What better time than now?

"Knock it off!" A fellow with more sense slammed a hand down on the shoulder of the furious man who looked ready to throw himself across the circle. "You know why we're here. This is business, and it's our job to finish it."

"What do you suggest we do that we haven't?" someone asked.

Cam, she saw, hadn't gotten sucked entirely into the drama. His rifle held in firing position, he was slowly turning his head, eyes narrowed. His lips had thinned, his face lacking any expression whatsoever. She, too, should have been aware that the group in front of them might not be relaxed enough to talk and argue if they hadn't sent out sentries. Whether they'd heard from Reggie Davis at some point or not, they must guess he hadn't succeeded in his mission to steer the search party wrong— or kill them.

Mara closed her eyes, breathed deeply, then focused on what she could see around the men. Packs, singly or tossed in a pile. A few rifles leaned carelessly against boulders. Clothes draped over rocks and packs.

And yes, more pieces of metal, torn like paper. Mysterious chunks and shreds she couldn't identify, most too small to answer any questions.

No other body.

Not a body, she told herself, seeking calm: Brianna.

She tugged her binoculars from inside her outermost layer of fleece and lifted them cautiously. No one was looking this way. She studied the faces she could see, recognizing three of them. She didn't know any of them well, but she'd seen them around town. Probably at the tavern. So…likely construction workers from the resort.

Not wanting to risk anyone catching a glint of the sun off glass—if that was possible with this dense canopy— she left the strap around her neck, but tucked the binoculars back in place in case she had to run.

Cam signaled her again, then continued slowly across the downslope she swore was getting steeper. She tried to place each foot as carefully as he did. Thank God the moss wasn't wet, or their passage might not be possible. Instinctively, she tipped her head to look up, but if any rain clouds were gathering, they were blocked by the ancient forest.

Like Cam, she searched their surroundings. Other parts of the airplane could be anywhere.

He stopped so suddenly, she took a couple of steps closer to him before she could do the same. Her gaze followed his pointing finger.

A single seat, entirely intact, stuck out from more

crumpled metal. One side of the seat belt dangled, while the other was missing. Mara pictured herself walking toward the creek and climbing onto that seat. She thought it was low enough she could do that. If that had been Bri's seat…she could have survived, couldn't she? If the seat belt held until near the very end? Although it wasn't apparent what had happened to the roof of the cabin, or the floor, for that matter.

A sudden splash had her tensing. A dark shape slipped through the water before diving. A beaver. Now that she was looking, the dam constructed of sticks was obvious.

Cam had just taken a photo with his phone, she saw. Tucking it away, he moved forward. Somehow they'd dropped closer to the creek than she'd realized. Not exactly by choice; he'd found what had to be a game trail that meandered above the creek. It certainly wasn't flat, but was slightly more comfortable to walk on.

Something brushed her neck and cheek and made her spin in alarm. It was nothing but a wispy strand of pale green lichen, but now her heart was trying to explode out of her chest.

If Bri had been in that seat, if she were alive—what would she have done?

Gone looking for her mother, Mara realized immediately. How had she dealt with the horror if she'd found Diana? And wow. Mara made a face. She was making a whole lot of assumptions here. If Bri had been in that particular seat, her body could have been cast anywhere within an acre or more. And…a human body wasn't nearly as strong as metal. It could be torn to pieces, too.

Mara's stomach rolled.

She had to close her eyes and breathe slowly for a moment. She knew better than to speculate like this. Cam was setting an example she needed to follow. Stay aware at all times; study the surroundings; do *not* allow emotions to distract her.

She pushed back at the resentment, because *he* didn't love the one person who was still missing after the crash.

A GRUNT SOMEWHERE behind Cam fired up instincts that too readily flung him back into wartime. Although this *was* war, in a different way. They'd covered some ground, but was this one of the sentries?

He swung around, bracing himself on one of the ubiquitous tree trunks, and saw Mara just appearing behind him. Her head turned, and he thought he saw panic on her face.

Was somebody following them? He'd have sworn they hadn't been seen earlier.

Low limbs on a cedar whipped sideways, and what emerged wasn't human. It was a black bear, and a big one, his head swinging as he searched for whatever alien smell had caught his attention. He wasn't ten feet behind Mara, who stood right on the trail.

For an instant, none of them moved. Then the bear charged straight ahead. Cam's hand dropped to his weapon, but he knew better. There wasn't time anyway, and a bullet would be like a bee sting to a black bear this size.

Mara tried to move sideways, but her foot slid. The bear never changed his trajectory. His shoulder slammed into her, sending her flying. He brushed past Cam, who breathed in a rank smell even as he tried to rush back to Mara—who wasn't where he'd last seen her.

He all but threw himself at the tree that was closest and swung himself around it. God—there she was, unmoving, twisted, easily ten feet downslope. She must have hit another of the massive trees headfirst. Had she broken her neck?

Swearing under his breath, Cam descended to Mara as fast as he could go and still stay on his feet. There, he dropped to his knees just below her, where he could see her face.

A faint groan didn't reassure him.

"Mara," he said, gently touching her cheek.

She whimpered. Her lashes fluttered, and then her lids rose to reveal dazed eyes. "Wha—?"

"You took the fast way downhill." He slid his fingers into her hair but came up against the tree before he could detect any goose egg. "Don't move."

Her indecipherable noise might have been intended to be a laugh.

"I want to get the pack off you, but first, let me see you wriggle your fingers."

The pause was excruciating, but then the fingers on the one hand he could see flexed and almost balled into a fist.

"Good. How do your feet feel?"

"Ache."

Some of the tension in his body let loose. His head dropped forward, and his shoulders slumped.

"Okay. Let me do the work. Don't try to sit up yet." He eased his hand beneath the padded strap on one side and was able to slide it down only a short way. How the hell was he going to get the thing off her without wrenching both arms backward?

Inch by inch, that was how. He was just starting to lift it off when she mumbled, "Neck hurts. Can I move?"

"Not yet." Her pack weighed as much as some he'd carried during deployments. As *she* would have carried, too, he realized. The weight was more than most women would even think about heaving onto their backs. He laid it down, realized he still carried his own and slid it off to sit beside hers.

Still on his knees beside her, he said quietly, "All right, sweetheart. Let's move you slowly. Okay? I'm going to support your neck."

Despite his effort to move her a fraction of an inch at a time, she squirmed a little to straighten her neck. Blood soaked into the bark of the tree where her head had hit.

"Better," she mumbled, rolled her shoulders a little and started to gather herself to rise.

"Take it easy. You hit that tree like a projectile."

"Tell me about it." She got her knees and elbows beneath herself, and gradually shifted to a sitting position. "Olympic dive. All tens. 'Cept for the landing."

She wasn't dead. She wasn't paralyzed. She could make a joke. He was still stuck in the horror of seeing how she'd landed.

The right side of her face was bloody and already swelling. The biggest lump, he wasn't surprised to find, was on her head. She really had slammed into the tree. Thank heavens they were far enough from the grumbling men not to have drawn attention.

He dug in his pack for first aid supplies, first gently cleaning the blood off her face and soaking some of it out of her hair so he could see what injuries lay beneath it. That eye was half swollen shut.

"Bet you have a black eye," he told her.

She snorted. Very softly, obviously not wanting to use her facial muscles any more than she had to.

Her face was scraped. Maybe had slid over the trunk until the top of her head connected. If so, that might have eased the dangerous strain on her neck.

He massaged her neck and shoulders, taking note of what hurt and what didn't. Then he asked what were no doubt irritating questions to determine whether she had suffered a concussion.

"Nuh-uh," she told him. "I'm…not fine, but okay."

He sank onto his butt. "You scared me."

"Scared me, too." She peered at him. "I thought he wanted to eat me."

"I think he was as scared as you were. There you were, something he didn't recognize, right in his path. I doubt he meant to hit you."

"No. Poor thing."

Cam wasn't feeling quite that forgiving just yet, but certainly she was right—the bear hadn't intended harm. "Big sucker," he observed.

"Almost time to hibernate. I have some ibuprofen," she added.

"So do I." He wanted to give her something stronger but didn't dare until he was sure she hadn't suffered significant damage to her brain. He shook a couple of pills from the bottle he carried in his first aid kit and offered them to her with his water to wash it down.

She tossed them in her mouth and washed them down, then sighed. "If you give me a few minutes, we can go on."

"The hell we can!" burst out of him before he could think.

She rested her head briefly against his shoulder in reassurance before saying, "We have to."

She was right, but he didn't have to like it.

THEY LOST PROBABLY an hour before Cam was reassured enough to concede they could move. Their pace was now so slow, she could have crawled almost as fast, but Mara was grateful. Her head throbbed in time with her heartbeat, and her neck really hurt. She had a bad feeling that by morning she wouldn't be able to turn her head at all. But she had to stay alert! Be observant.

Cam led again but didn't allow any space to open between them. He scanned their surroundings even more carefully than before, obviously aware that she wouldn't be able to do the same.

The forest gradually came back to life. Birds fell briefly silent as the humans passed, squirrels peered bright-eyed at them, and low, lacy boughs on cedar trees fluttered as something small moved beneath them.

A couple of times, Cam paused to point out more shreds of Dennis's beloved Beechcraft.

Where could Bri be?

Cam abruptly stopped, and she ran into him. The impact, slight though it was, rattled her brain and she had to close her eyes for a moment. When she opened them, it was to a shocking sight: another seat still attached to a good-size section of plane, although it was twisted enough she couldn't quite imagine how Bri would have survived if she'd been sitting in it.

But this was the rear of the plane. There was the tail,

intact if lying sideways—and a gaping maw that had to be the luggage compartment. A quiver ran through Mara. Cam gripped her upper arm as if afraid she'd dash from cover.

Binoculars. Mara pulled them out, vaguely aware that Cam was doing the same. The compartment appeared completely empty, but a jumble of bags and clothes and things she couldn't identify was strewn in front of it. Would everything have fallen out like that?

"They've dug through it all," Cam murmured.

Yes. Still Mara stared. A suitcase she recognized—Diana's—was completely open and looked like someone had smashed it up and down a few times. Bri's duffel bag, a swirl of purple and pink, was mixed in with everything else but looked limp as if whatever it had held had been dumped out. A cardboard box was flattened. Most pilots carried things like bottled water, a sleeping bag or blanket, packaged foods like energy bars that were edible for a long time. Surely Dennis did the same, if only to reassure nervous passengers. *See? We're all set if we go down and have to wait for rescue.* The fact that he carried supplies like that implied his confidence that the plane wouldn't *crash*; there just was an unlikely possibility that he'd have to set it down somewhere unexpected.

The men might have taken the food and any other supplies, she thought, but wasn't sure why they'd have bothered given the hefty packs she'd seen sitting around the small clearing. Certainly, food kept in cargo would likely be stale at best.

What would Dennis have brought in his own duffel bag? Increasingly hopeful, she didn't actually see it. Clothes, yes. He liked some really gaudy T-shirts that usually had sort of funny but obscene sayings on them. Mostly khaki cargo pants; a leg from one of them was wrapped around Bri's duffel.

One of Bri's tennis shoes appeared to have been flung aside. She wore those most of the time, and probably would have when her mother dragged her along on this outing. Otherwise, Mara couldn't see much that would have belonged to Bri. No sleeping bag or blanket, either. Nothing that looked like Dennis's brown duffel bag.

"I wish we could go dig through all that," she whispered.

"Not a chance."

"No, I know, but—" Hope was almost choking her.

"We need to get farther away. Then we can talk. I have to use the radio, too."

Mara bobbed her head, even though she could hardly tear her gaze from the heap of clothing and miscellaneous items. A splash of color had to be Diana's cosmetic bag. If she kept looking… But instead she followed him obediently, as if she was trapped in the draft of Cam's passage. Even so, she did her best to look around until she tripped.

She gave herself a mental slap. She wouldn't be any good to Bri if she got hurt again, maybe worse, or brought one of the bad guys down on them.

Cam crossed the game trail this time, heading what felt like straight up the ridge. The angle of trees to ground grew increasingly sharp, the effect surreal. He used low branches of cedar to hoist himself, always waiting while she did the same. When she couldn't reach, he'd take her hand and gently tug her up. Her thighs burned, her head throbbed, and her pack tried to drag her backward.

Her thoughts jumbled. Who did he intend to call? The

original SAR members? Or the HRT… No, he said they wouldn't respond to something like this. Some kind of tactical team that would undoubtedly carry weapons at least as deadly as those she'd seen leaning against rocks and packs.

But what if they came in shooting, and Bri was there somewhere, held captive? She'd die, that's what.

If Cam called only the park law enforcement rangers who'd headed north when they split up, or Lori Holmes and Dr. Dan, Mara and he would have to wait and wait, and they'd still be outnumbered.

The hope she had held onto so hard curdled, leaving her scared, hurting and feeling powerless.

# Chapter Thirteen

Bri couldn't remember the last time she'd actually seen the sky. It felt colder now than it had yesterday, too, but that might only be because she wasn't moving. It was too early in the fall to snow, wasn't it?

The most she'd done once it was light enough was find a shirt in the duffel bag and sort of tie it in a circle so she could drop it around her neck and use it like a sling. She wasn't sure her arm hurt any less, but it might keep her from scraping the ends of broken bones together.

Even with her mouth so dry, she ate first a tasteless energy bar, then a candy bar. Swallowing wasn't easy. She almost wished it would rain, except what if it *kept* raining until the well around this tree started filling with water? Well/water. Aunt Mara would say that was a pun. Bri didn't always get the puns that made her aunt laugh. This one didn't feel funny, either.

She dug out her bottle for about the dozenth time since she'd fallen into this hole. The bottle was still just as empty. Sooner or later, she'd have to find water. During the spring and early summer, there would have been streams from melting snow tumbling down to the river. Bri remembered staring for the longest time at a miniature waterfall. Even small streams found their way around obstacles.

Thinking about running water made her mouth feel even more parched.

The trouble was, she'd climbed a long way up. Going down might be even harder, especially hurting so much and not being able to use one of her hands to brace herself on tree trunks or catch hold of small branches. Moss was a really weird surface to walk on. Kind of cushiony, but also easy to tear up, so if she wasn't really, really careful, she'd fall on her butt and slide. Maybe even hit a tree and break more bones.

Plus, if she made it all the way down there, she just knew she'd be seen. She hadn't seen or heard anyone since…she couldn't remember exactly. Midafternoon? How could they ever find her here? But if she showed herself crouching beside the creek to fill her water bottle, someone would see her.

People did die from thirst, like in the desert, but she didn't have sun baking down on her. Dying would have to take a long time. A couple of days, at least?

What if she heard Aunt Mara calling for her, and her mouth was too dry to answer?

Even scarier was wondering how Aunt Mara *would* find her. This forest went on forever and ever, the trees looking so much the same, and it was so steep up here. Nobody could see her from above, like from a helicopter. Eventually she'd have to try to pull herself out of her hidey-hole and go back down to the creek, trusting the bad guys had given up and were gone.

Only, how long would it be before that happened?

Oh, why did she hide the money?

HEARING THE OCCASIONAL tiny whimper or groan that Mara couldn't hold back was killing Cam. She should be getting an MRI, not lugging that monstrous pack while she scrambled up a mountain.

He stopped sooner than he'd have liked but was mostly satisfied that nobody could be near. Unless they'd been seen, what were the odds of anybody stumbling on them? Particularly since he seriously doubted any of the men the traffickers had rounded up for this expedition had any background in mountain climbing or exploring untracked forest.

Bri didn't, either, he reminded himself, but desperation was a powerful motivator.

The downed tree that he had hoped would provide a seat was more rotten than he would have liked. After he lifted Mara's pack from her back and helped her sit, he heard a crumbly sound. Nonetheless, he swung his own pack off and joined her. Yeah, he was compressing the rotten wood beneath him, but at this point, taking the weight off his feet felt better than the big leather recliner he had in his condo. And if he felt such profound relief, what about Mara?

He studied her, seeing strain, a few small tracks that might be from tears or only sweat and creases in her forehead. He hadn't gotten all the blood, either; her hair on the one side was stiff with dried blood, and smears decorated her discolored, swollen face.

Damn. If only he had a way to send her home.

His mouth twisted. Who was he kidding? He'd have to tie her up to get her on a helicopter, assuming he could wish one up.

She half turned her upper body so that her pleading

eyes could meet his. "I think Bri is alive. Most of the stuff missing from the cargo area is either hers or things she might have thought she'd need."

"I hope you're right," he said quietly. "I didn't believe there was any chance at all, but... I'm changing my mind."

He'd been weighing explanations for the group of men lurking for days around a crashed small plane—one that had been driven down. They had to be searching for something. The question was why they couldn't find it. If the plane broke up midair, smaller contents could have been strewn over many acres. But the fact that the parts of the plane were all in a relatively confined area argued against that. If the item was tiny, as he'd conjectured before, what were the odds anyone would ever find it? If it was information, surely it could be replaced.

If Terrell had been missing, him grabbing whatever it was and going on the run would make sense, but Cam didn't have to see him up close to know that Dennis Terrell was definitely dead.

"Why would Brianna take whatever they need so much?" he heard himself ask.

"She's always snooping into her mom's business. Diana gets really mad at her." Mara swallowed. "What if she heard them talking about whatever it is?"

That was a possibility.

He didn't ask how she thought a slight girl had been able to emerge from the wreckage able to go on the run. And yet, as an explanation, it increasingly filled in the blanks.

He knew the two adults on the Beechcraft were dead. If the men had found Brianna's body, why would they have hidden it? Or would they do something like throw it in the water to save themselves from the unpleasant knowledge that they'd killed a child?

Maybe.

He, too, suspected that they'd rummaged through the luggage, most of which would be of no use whatsoever to them. The only obvious thing he'd seen that had to be Brianna's was the pink and purple duffel bag, but if her aunt was to be believed, she was a smart kid. She would have known better than to carry something so easy to spot in these woods.

Radiating anxiety, Mara was still watching him.

"We've got only a couple of options," he said at last. "We can discuss them once I find out what's happened with the rest of our party—and check in with the tactical team."

Her head bobbed.

He started with Brent Hallquist.

Hallquist answered immediately. "Agent Frasier? Thank God. We've been worrying about your silence."

Cam explained that he'd gone silent once he had suspected he and Mara were close to the crash site. "In fact, we were. We've inspected it as well as we can, given that there are a minimum of eight to ten men essentially camped there."

"Eight or ten?" Mara mouthed.

He shook his head at her. "The pilot and the woman who was beside him in the cockpit are dead. We didn't have to get any closer to tell. What we do know is that the men are searching for something or someone. We've found no sign of Brianna Dawson. I don't know how she could have survived, but if she did, she'd have known the crash was no accident. She's smart enough to hide. She's done some hiking and backpacking with her aunt, and hiding out here shouldn't be difficult." He paused. "Update me. What about Joe Walden?"

"Unconscious when we found him. He's on his feet and hiking with us now. I'd like to get him to a hospital, which is why we're presently following Baker River toward the lake."

If Cam's memory of the map was accurate, trails, campgrounds and even a resort surrounded the lake. "Okay. What about the doctor and Deputy Holmes?"

The doctor had treated the pilot. They'd made the decision for her, after treatment, to fly back to headquarters. The park service didn't have extra helicopters or pilots hanging around. He and the deputy had reluctantly chosen to go with her, since by that time they assumed they were too far away from Cam and Mara's location to be any help.

"Okay." Cam paused to think. "Call Deputy Walker in Thunder Creek. Ask him to go talk to Dave Simmons at the resort. It would be interesting to know if he's directing the men out here or if he's been replaced." Or permanently indisposed, but Cam didn't say that. "If Terrell stole something, that means it was left lying around. Pretty careless. Simmons seems likely to have been the one responsible."

"You'd think they'd have ransacked Terrell's house early on, too, wouldn't you?" the ranger said thoughtfully.

"I'd put money on it."

"Okay. Let me know anything else we can do—or if you want us to deliver Joe and then rejoin you and Ms. Dawson."

Cam agreed to stay in touch. He'd have been glad to have the rangers, but two more men wasn't enough to give him the upper hand. Since he had jurisdiction here as much as they did, that wasn't an issue. This was federal land, and he was a federal agent, as would be the tactical team who responded.

He did speak to their dispatcher, who gave him the bad news that the team was no longer waiting to be summoned. They'd been needed in Idaho where an attempted arrest of a couple of domestic terrorists had led to a shootout and a credible bomb threat.

"They haven't forgotten your problem."

Big of them, Cam couldn't help thinking. Out of the corner of his eye, he saw Mara's lips part, but she didn't say anything.

The dispatcher continued, "Collins told me that once the ATF shows up on scene to analyze the likelihood of bombs or joins local law enforcement and a SWAT team to free up his team, they'll return straight to Bellingham."

"All right. I'm not quite ready for them anyway. I'm hoping by tomorrow I'll be in a better position here."

The moment he stowed the radio, Mara asked, "What will be any different tomorrow?"

"They might have given up and left the site to us."

He watched her absorb that, the pain in her expressive eyes not diminishing at all. "What are we going to do in the meantime?"

"Move a little closer again."

She was desperate to take action, and he sympathized. He was itching to make a move, too, specifically to hunt for that little girl. Cam suspected he'd had more practice in stomping out the slow burn of frustration.

"That's *all*?" Amazing that she had still kept her voice low.

"What do you suggest?" He didn't intend that as sarcasm or a put-down, and her expression didn't indicate she was taking it that way. He would love to hear it if she had a better idea.

"What I want is to look for Bri." She compressed her lips. "I just…can't think how we can do that without drawing attention."

"We can't walk around calling her name, that's for sure. If she's hiding, I can't think of anything else that would bring her out."

"No."

"Hey," he said, and took the chance of wrapping his arm around Mara's shoulders.

For a moment she stayed stiff, but just as he was thinking he should give her a quick hug and withdraw his arm, she collapsed against him. Mara pressed her face against his shoulder and grabbed a handful of his shirt with her free hand. And then…she shook.

Apparently she trusted him enough, at least, to have an emotional breakdown.

It had to be several minutes before the tension in her muscles seemed to drain away, and while she continued to lean against him, her shoulders sagged and her fist loosened.

Cam had already bowed his head to look down at her, but now he laid his cheek against her ruffled hair. Stubble that was rapidly becoming a short beard caught in her hair, but he didn't lift his head. Holding her calmed him.

The minutes ticked by. He realized he was rocking slightly, a wordless attempt to comfort her.

"Oh!" she exclaimed suddenly. "I *hate* not being able to do anything."

"Me, too," he admitted. If he hadn't been driven by a need to be in charge, to take action, he wouldn't have chosen first the army and then the FBI. Being forced to wait was inevitable, of course, and while he was good at hiding how he felt, that didn't mean he wasn't as frustrated as she was.

No, that was wrong. She might as well be Brianna Dawson's mother, which meant she'd be in an agony of suspense and had been all along. He shouldn't have let her join the search party, but if it had been the other way around, he'd have been enraged to be excluded. As it was, Mara had held her emotions in check enough to follow direction, lead when he suggested it and back him up when his life had been on the line. She was a remarkable woman, one he didn't want to have to say goodbye to when the time came for him to return to the Seattle office.

His usual confidence in himself wasn't high, given that she already felt he'd betrayed her, but he wanted to believe she had set that aside. If she didn't trust him, would she let him hold her like this?

Naturally, that was the moment she gathered herself and retreated, although he'd swear she released his shirt slowly enough to give away some reluctance. She flattened her hand and smoothed the wrinkles out before sitting up straight and squeezing her hands together on her lap.

Her cheeks were pink, too, he saw with interest. She looked shy when she finally met his eyes.

"I'm sorry."

"You have nothing to be sorry for. Not being able to find Brianna and have some answers has to be getting to you in a big way. I wish—" He put the brakes on.

"You wish?"

His lips twisted into a sort of rueful smile. "The same things you wish." Except he also wished she'd begun imagining him as part of her future. Cam was shocked enough to be thinking that way about a woman with whom he hadn't even had a real relationship.

She bit her lip and turned her head so he was looking at her profile. "So…now what?"

He rolled his shoulders and heard a couple of pops. "Lunch," he said. "It's got to be noon." He pushed up his sleeve. "No, one thirty. Then we'll retrace our steps and place ourselves where we can see as much as possible without being discovered."

"I'm not—"

"Eat anyway."

Her scathing look was reassuring. That was the spirited woman who drew him, the one who refused to back down.

Her "fine" was snippy enough to help pull him out of the gooey morass of emotions he'd indulged in.

When she opened a large pocket on the outside of her pack and started rummaging for food, he was glad not to have to do any bullying.

# Chapter Fourteen

Even screened by low evergreen boughs and fern fronds, Cam and Mara had a bird's eye view of most of the crash site. She hadn't argued when he led the way to what he considered the best cover that allowed the view. He might not have a lot of experience in the north Cascades, but he moved with the arrogant grace of the cougars that made their home in this forest. Strategic thinking seemed equally effortless for him.

Even if she'd disagreed with his decision about where to stop, she wouldn't have. She was too emotionally invested, and she knew it.

They agreed then to take turns watching. Right now, she was scanning as much of the riverbank and wreckage as she could with her binoculars, while he sat with his legs outstretched and his back against a cedar. He'd had to break off a few low, feathery branches to make room for his wide shoulders and height, but had done so without making much noise.

A couple of times, some men had walked within thirty yards or so of them—close enough to bring whichever one of them was on break to a crouch—but not seen them. At first, Mara thought they were just astonishingly unobservant, but finally decided they had already searched all the closest and most accessible forest, so were just passing through without it occurring to them they might not be alone here anymore.

She'd shaken her head at the thought, catching Cam's attention, but he didn't ask any questions. In fact, neither had said a word since they'd hunkered down here.

Voices drifted to them from time to time. The tone was invariably irritated if not outright angry. Which she might be, too, although she couldn't say she sympathized. Still, whoever had let Dennis stroll away with whatever he'd stolen probably wasn't here. *These* men weren't directly responsible, but they were the ones who had to crash around in unfamiliar terrain, turn ankles, get scratches across their faces and lower arms, slip and fall hard enough to acquire bruises. Of course, they'd sold out to scum in the first place for some bigger bucks.

She'd heard a few obscenities that were new ones for her. She might have been amused if her anger and fear weren't always at a simmer.

Suddenly a man snarled, "That kid must be part mountain goat."

Yes!

Hope swelled again as if enough helium had been pumped into her chest to allow her to rise from the ground. She turned to look at Cam, who'd raised his eyebrows and was grinning.

Oh God, Bri was alive!

For all Mara's exhilaration, the helium seeped out. She couldn't stop herself from imagining everything else besides dying in the crash that could have happened to a young girl in an untracked wilderness. She might look like a meal to a cougar, or...or had stumbled on a bear's den. Fatal falls were always possible. And…had she found any food? It had been cold enough last night Bri might have been in trouble without a sleeping bag or heavy parka.

Mara stopped herself. No. Bri had survived the crash. She was alive and smart enough to stay ahead of all these blockheads stumbling through the woods and carrying on conversations with voices that carried a long way. How *did* they expect to find her?

*Crack.* The sound of a single shot brought her to her feet.

Cam was suddenly at her side, gripping her hand. "Rifle," he murmured. "East of here. Higher elevation."

Several men in the vicinity grabbed their own rifles and disappeared into the forest to find out what had happened.

Cam and Mara waited, Mara thinking frantically. Bri wouldn't have a weapon unless she'd repurposed a branch into a club. Why would anyone have fired at her? They couldn't be hunting this hard with no purpose but killing her. That made no sense; what could she possibly know that was so damaging to them?

Mara knew quite well that she was protecting herself. Who knew why any of this had happened? If Bri was carrying whatever it was that they sought, killing her might seem reasonable. In that case, they wouldn't need her alive, only to be able to search her.

Mara realized she was praying. Cam's hand tightened on hers until his grip was almost painful, but she didn't mind. She needed the connection, drank in the hard, predatory expression on his face. As grateful as she was for his skill, his strength, his ability to strategize, not to mention the prior intelligence he'd drawn on and the forces he could command, she had long since forgiven him for pretending to be someone he wasn't when they first met.

Mara was glad not to have a watch to count the agonizingly slow minutes. She had to remind herself to breathe. If Cam was breathing, she couldn't tell.

Voices shouted through the woods again. "Idiot" was one of the few words she picked up.

Finally, two men passed frighteningly close. Thank God neither so much as turned his head.

"A bear," one of them growled. "Like the damn thing was going to hurt him! Will he shoot at the next squirrel that scampers by? Ridley is going to be steamed."

"If someone reports hearing gunfire, cops or rangers or somebody will be on us like stink on—"

Mara couldn't hear the rest but didn't need to.

"Wonder who Ridley is?" Cam said quietly.

*A bear.* She twisted enough to hug Cam. Just a bear. They hadn't found Bri.

His arms closed around her. "Hope the shot didn't hit the bear."

She did, too, but someone who panicked that easily wasn't likely to be a crack shot. And honestly, a bear like the one that had sent her flying was unlikely to be brought down by a single bullet anyway.

"I'll take over," Cam added and gently eased her away.

She sank to the loam and moss where he'd been sitting and pulled her knees up so she could hug them.

THE CRACK OF a gunshot yanked Bri out of her half sleep, half stupor. The involuntary jerk sent pain ripping through her.

Who? Where?

It was too close, she knew that, but she'd have heard the bullet strike her tree. Shredded bark would have rained down. Had whoever fired the shot thought he'd seen *her*? As awful as all of this was, she hadn't imagined they would shoot her as if she were a deer they were bagging. No, it had to be the duffel they still wanted. Her brain wasn't working very well, but she knew that much.

If she just stayed where she was, she'd be safe. Except she was trembling, feeling achy all over and so, so thirsty. Cold, too, she realized, even though this was the heat of the day. Maybe…maybe one of her injuries was infected.

If she stayed where she was…she might die here.

If they didn't find her, she'd keep getting thirstier and thirstier, and sicker and sicker. She'd hit her head, too, so she didn't know whether to blame the pain or the fear or something worse for her muddled thinking.

She desperately wanted to hear a voice she knew calling her name, but was that even possible if men carrying rifles were still searching the woods?

Closing her eyes, she wiped tears and snot on the knees of her jeans and rocked herself. Why weren't those men calling her name? Did they not know it? And… would she have been foolish enough, early on, to show herself if some guy had called out for her?

No.

*Stay*, she told herself. *Stay, stay.* What good would wandering on do?

Twilight arrived suddenly, between one blink of the eye and the next. That was the way it happened in the mountains. The moment the sun sank behind the tallest peak, dusk fell in the mountain's shadow.

Mara was on guard when she noticed several men emerging separately from the woods in a short time frame. Two more appeared on the other side of the creek, running low enough in late fall that they could just splash across. That side of the V of the valley rose so steeply, she hadn't known the search had extended there—or that Bri would have thought for a minute that that was her best option for hiding. Still…earlier she'd noticed a slice of white metal leaning against a boulder on the far side. These guys were getting desperate.

If only there'd been nearby trails where Bri could have stumbled on hikers or climbers who would have helped her.

Of course, those kind hikers could have been gunned down.

A hand squeezed Mara's shoulder, and she jumped.

"I think we might want to get a little farther away before we bed down."

"No!" burst out of her.

He covered her mouth with that big hand. "Hush. Nothing is going to happen now. We need to eat and get some sleep."

Tears burned at the back of Mara's eyes, but she wouldn't let them fall. She'd revealed too much weakness to this man already. So she made herself nod and climb to her feet.

He already held her pack so that she could easily insert her arms beneath the straps. What's more, he had his own pack on, and she hadn't even noticed! What kind of guard was she?

Cam set out with his usual, automatic assumption that she'd follow. Which she did, because he was skilled at finding what they needed. She didn't remember noticing anyplace that would allow two people to lay out sleeping bags.

His path this time took them at a slant, causing them to lurch with each step. And, sure enough, not twenty minutes later, he murmured, "This should work."

That fast, it was getting hard to see. She had to blink a couple of times before she saw a fallen nurse log and the alcove behind it. The rotting tree wasn't just housing the roots of new trees, it was probably also home to a bunch of creepy crawlies. But none in this area were poisonous, and as they'd munched and tunneled, something much like sawdust lay on the far side.

Cam scraped the soil with his boots, leveling it further. Mara lowered herself to her knees and freed herself from the pack again. In silence, both laid out thin pads and their sleeping bags. He produced a camp stove.

Who would see the tiny flame? The idea of a hot dinner in her stomach raised her flagging spirits.

They ate the vegetarian chili quietly, Mara sitting cross-legged, Cam leaning against the nurse log, those long legs outstretched. It wasn't pitch dark yet but getting there.

After scraping her bowl bare, she asked, "Will they ever give up?"

He moved his shoulders as if expressing discomfort rather than an answer. His voice was low, husky. "They've been more persistent than I would have expected."

"Did you notice anybody who looked like they were

in charge?" She dug out a candy bar and offered him a second one.

He tore it open. "Not obviously so. They wouldn't whine as much as they have if the big boss was there, but somebody has to be responsible for directing their movements."

"They must have radios."

"That's my take."

"Do you suppose they reported that one of their guys fired a rifle because a bear startled him?"

She couldn't clearly make out his face anymore, but the humor in his voice rang clear as he said, "I doubt it. *I* wouldn't have."

Her laugh surprised her. She thought she'd forgotten how to laugh.

Cam lifted his bottle and shook it. "I have enough for coffee now, or in the morning. Unless you have more water—?"

"Let me check." They'd refilled when they crossed a stream descending from the ridge—or was it a mountain?—midday. She held it out. "I have plenty."

"Then you haven't been drinking enough," he said sternly.

He was right. She excused herself because they had mostly been sitting today, but getting dehydrated was dangerous. She held out the bottle. "I vote for coffee now and in the morning."

His chuckle was deep and quiet. Mara imagined the vibration in his chest that produced it. What would that feel like if her hand rested on that chest? She wished…oh, she wished for so much, and that made her mad at herself when she should be thinking about only one person: Bri.

Neither said anything as they waited for the water to boil. Only when Cam handed her a cup of coffee and she inhaled its rich scent did he say, "I didn't think your niece could have survived."

"I know." She closed her eyes for a moment. "No one thought so."

He grunted. "Except maybe Davis. He really hauled ass to catch up to us. At the very least, he knew how stirred up the men here were."

"You didn't see a second radio in his pack."

She thought Cam shook his head.

"I could have looked more thoroughly, though. In my defense, I didn't want to hang around his body. He was talking pretty loudly. Did you notice?"

Mara crinkled her forehead. "No, but I was mostly concentrating on not making any noise myself."

Another of those chuckles made her tingle.

They sipped in more silence, until he asked, "Did Terrell buy the house they were in?"

Well, that was a jump in topic. "No, I'm sure neither of them did. It's one reason I'm renting, too. I couldn't imagine Diana staying happy in such a remote, small town."

"And if she moved, you moved."

"That made her mad, but yes."

After a pause, he said quietly, "You must be relieved."

Mara swallowed a lump in her throat. "I want to be relieved, but…what if Bri is injured? How could she *not* have been injured? Just because they can't find her body close by doesn't mean—" She couldn't say it.

He reached out and took her hand in that way he did,

the warmth and strength reassurance she couldn't remember anyone offering her in a very long time.

If ever. Unless she was very wrong, she could easily love the man Cam Frasier had proved himself to be.

For a skeptic, that was a silly thing to think.

"I studied what was left around the cargo hold," he said, obviously unaware of the direction of her thoughts, "and I think you're right. Not much that was hers seemed to have been left. If she was able to locate that part of the plane, sort through the bags and clothes and understand that she had to open some distance from the wreckage, she was doing okay."

Mara sniffed. *No crying*, she ordered herself. "I think the first thing she'd have done was try to find her mom. And Dennis, except I wonder how much she saw when the plane went down."

"I wonder, too. From all reports, Terrell was a skilled pilot."

She frowned. "They couldn't exactly have bumped his fender, the way a car could push another one off the road."

"That's what I'm thinking. Once he realized he couldn't shake them, why wouldn't he have headed for monitored airspace? Would he really have preferred to kill himself, Diana and Bri rather than maybe getting a short jail term?"

"Short?"

"He'd have had to be upfront about what was going on at the resort and what he'd been expected to do. I think prosecutors would have happily swapped time he should have served for a witness against the bosses."

"Would it have been that easy?"

"If he'd landed right away and gone straight to law enforcement, yeah." Briefly, his voice had gone hard, in a way familiar to Mara.

"So…so why do you think he crashed?" she asked.

"I'm guessing gunshots. Chances are good we'll find bullets or other evidence once the techs get their hands on the wreckage."

"You don't think all those men haven't cleaned house?"

He let out a distinct snort. "You saw the debris. How could they manage that?"

Thinking it over, Mara frowned. "Will it be the FBI that lays claim to the wreckage?"

"Ah, can't be sure. You know the National Transportation Safety Board is all over pretty well any plane or helicopter that goes down." His arm moved in a shrug. "We usually get along well enough. In this case, that crash was no accident."

"No."

He was the one to suggest they get ready to bed down. When he released her hand to stand up, Mara felt the loss. She had enough aches and pains, she didn't rise to her feet with any of the grace he had. She bumped into a tree trunk she couldn't see and stumbled over a rock or who knew what in her effort to achieve some privacy.

They both brushed their teeth, then shed outer layers of clothes to slide into their sleeping bags. Mara touched her handgun to make sure it was close enough and assumed Cam kept his near, too. His rifle leaned against his pack within reach.

She needed to sleep but lay on her back staring straight up into the darkness, her body rigid. Faint sounds came to her: a whisper from high in the trees, as those branches bent before a breeze; a hoot from not far above her, and a few rustles closer to ground level.

When Cam moved, she heard the slippery sound of his sleeping bag. What was he—?

Very quietly, he said, "I wish we were in a bed so I could hold you."

Did he mean to be comforting, or was this a declaration?

Her mouth opened and closed. Finally, she had to admit, "I think I'd like that."

"C'mere." He reached out a long arm and tugged her, sleeping bag and all, until she lay tucked up to him. She tensed again until he said softly, "Relax. You need to sleep."

"I… Won't you get cold?" That arm was bare, although she felt the thin T-shirt when she laid her head on the curve just below his shoulder. Still no bare skin.

"No," he said huskily.

He didn't have to move far to press his lips to her forehead. Those lips were as soft as his voice. She'd have liked to lift her own hand to lay it on his face, but her sleeping bag held her captive.

After a silence, he said, "Except for not telling you who I was, I didn't fake anything. I hope you can believe that."

She wanted him to kiss her, but encouraging that would have felt like a betrayal when Bri was still missing. Still scared, whether she was hurt or not.

But Mara did whisper, "I do. You had no reason to trust me."

"Maybe not, but I never for a minute suspected you were mixed up in the mess I was investigating."

"Okay."

"Once we have Bri safe, I'm hoping you and I can start over again."

Her eyes stung again, but not with tears. She moved enough to rub her cheek against his chest. "The start we have is fine."

"Good."

That had to be another kiss on her forehead, but she was so relaxed, now she could sleep.

# Chapter Fifteen

Cam held himself very still when he first woke up, unsure whether something had disturbed him. Cheerful bird chatter reassured him, and he found the green-filtered light of early morning soothing. Somehow he'd come to be lying on his side, spooning a still sleeping Mara. More than ever, he regretted the thickness of two sleeping bags separating them. His lower body felt toasty, his shoulders and arms cold. Mara's head rested on his bicep, and his other arm was tucked around her, his hand close to cupping her breast.

"Rise and shine," he said in a low voice, although he felt sure they were still alone.

She groaned. "Is it already morning?"

"Afraid so."

Cam waited until she unzipped her sleeping bag and rolled off his arm.

"Brr!" She snatched her fleece quarter-zip, as he did the same.

Yeah, mornings felt increasingly cool. Was that possible in less than a week?

They had their morning routine down pat. Mara made oatmeal on her stove while he contributed a baggie full of raisins and then rolled her sleeping bag and pad for her. They sat side by side on his as they ate and then sipped coffee.

"So…what now?" she asked finally.

"I did some thinking last night," he said. "I'm assuming Bri is mobile."

For now, they had to make decisions based on the assumption that she had been able to walk away from the plane crash. He'd keep lingering doubts to himself.

"She also just about has to be injured," he added gently. "Scared for sure. What I figure is that the first thing she'd have done would be look for her mother."

The green in her eyes highlighted by their surroundings, Mara nodded.

"Once she found the cockpit with her mother and Terrell, what do you think she'd have done next? And let's assume she knows the plane didn't just fall out of the sky."

"She *has* to have seen the other plane chasing them, if nothing else. Plus… I'll bet Dennis was yelling."

Cam was betting that poor kid had seen considerably more than that, not to mention hearing some foul language, but he didn't say so.

"She'd be even more scared," Mara said slowly. "She had to realize that the people who'd made sure of the crash would know how to find the wreckage more easily than rescuers."

"Right. So she'd look for the cargo area of the plane."

"Uh-huh." Mara barely hesitated. "She knew she had to hide. I taught her the basics of what she'd need if she ever got lost or—"

No, she couldn't have foreseen anything like this.

"Thank God you did." He squeezed her free hand.

"Yes." She bit her lip. "So she packed a duffel—Dennis's, I think, because her own was too bright, and her mom's suitcase wasn't practical. I don't know whether Diana brought along any snacks or…or…"

"The odds are, Terrell carried supplies. Something like energy bars that stay edible for quite a while. A bottle of water. A sleeping bag or blanket. Pilots I've known always do."

"That…makes sense."

He didn't like seeing renewed fear on Mara's face, but he had to say this. "I think we're missing a step. Could she possibly have known *why* Terrell insisted on such an early departure? What he'd done that made him afraid?"

Mara made a face. No, he hadn't surprised her.

"I'm sure she didn't know the evening before. She'd have said something. Confronted her mother in front of us. Bri is mostly pretty direct."

"Bet her mother loved that."

Mara's smile was wry, but it *was* a smile. "Oh yeah." She fell silent for a moment, thinking. "Maybe she heard Diana and Dennis talking. Like I told you, she was nosy. And if it was late that night, what could she do? Her mother wasn't going to say, hey, you don't have to come if you don't want to."

"The question is, if she knew what Dennis had stolen, would she have ignored it after the crash?"

"No." Mara was almost whispering. "No. Not Bri. I don't know what she'd do—"

"Because we don't know what it was."

"Right. I think, if she could find a way to ruin it, like throw it in the creek, or stomp on it, she'd do it. Otherwise… she could have taken it with her."

"Or hidden it." The certainty had settled on him. "That's why they're hunting so hard for her. They think she has to know where their extremely valuable—or sensitive—possession is."

"Oh dear God. I'll bet that's what she did." All the strain she must be feeling was in an expression he'd almost call pleading.

Did she want him to say that wasn't what was happening? No, Mara was a woman who wouldn't appreciate a lie, however well meant it was. He'd learned his lesson on that.

But she was already continuing with quiet ferocity, "If someone killed Bri, I'd want to hurt them any way I could."

"Yeah, me, too." He'd only met Brianna Dawson once, although he had seen her around town or with Mara several other times. But a gutsy girl who'd lost her father early, had a mother who brought a string of probably unreliable men into their household, a mother she couldn't depend on the way she could her aunt… That Brianna had come to life for Cam.

And then he had to take into account the depth of his need to protect this woman, including the child she considered to be her own. He wanted to do more than hurt whoever was responsible for this ruthless hunt for a little girl—he wanted to hurt all the men who were apparently willing to do whatever it took to haul her in.

He would do anything to keep them from getting their hands on Brianna Dawson.

"So…what's the plan?" Mara asked him.

"Look for her ourselves," he said, but didn't add that he thought Bri's time was running out.

WHAT HAUNTED MARA was the next thing Cam said that morning. "Tomorrow, I'll have to bring in the tactical team."

Her mouth opened and closed, but he shook his head and said gently, "She can't hide forever, and they're showing no sign of being willing to pack up and leave, however big a risk they're taking with every extra day. What's this? Day five? Six? Everyone knows how intensive the hunt for a downed airplane is. It's only because of my involvement that the NTSB isn't here."

The end result of their talk was an agreement that it wouldn't have made sense for Bri to turn around, head east and pass the cockpit holding her dead mother again. Cam argued that her last stop at the wreckage would have been the cargo area. Pinned in the deep V of the river valley, Bri would likely have had no idea where she was or which way would be the easiest walking.

If she intended to hide, though, she'd surely have left the site as far behind as she could while orienting herself by the creek.

What they questioned was whether she could conceivably have crossed the creek.

Cam pulled out his map again, and they agreed that if she had reached the point where Lonesome Creek split from Bald Eagle, heading southward, that might have made sense. If she'd continued on Bald Eagle Creek, she'd have been heading directly toward Jupiter Pass and some seriously rugged country.

"Remember, she's not a hiker, strolling along," he'd pointed out. "She's on the run. I think she'd climb as high as she could get, where she'd be damned hard to find amid sizable timber."

Either way, they were going to split up.

"I can give you the radio I took from Davis," Cam said tightly.

She said the obvious. "We can't use the radios right now, anyway."

Cam grimaced. "Let's stay close enough to keep an eye on each other."

What they'd decided to do was shadow searchers who went out in the direction they'd decided was most logical. Once searchers gave up and turned back, Mara at least could quietly call for Bri.

*The best-made plans*, she thought unhappily, wishing again for...too many things, but mostly that they would stumble on Bri. And that was what it would just about take.

THE MORNING CHILL—or increased desperation—got the scumbags up early and on their way, spreading out immediately. A couple did cross the creek and push their way through the rampant if mostly leafless vegetation that grew from cracks between rocks. They'd probably been ordered to silence, but an occasional curse drifted from that direction.

The others, the ones who ghosted past Cam and Mara, knew better how to keep quiet. The moss helped, although he heard a few small branches break from careless footsteps.

They had initially intended to hide their packs and leave them behind instead of hindering themselves, but Cam decided he had to have his radio, another magazine of ammunition for his handgun, water bottle and some snack food, so he piled his extra clothes and sleeping bag next to her pack, while slinging first his much-reduced pack and then the rifle onto his back.

He could tell she hated leaving hers, but he said, "As long as one of us has some essentials."

She looked undecided but finally toed her pack beneath a cedar branch and added his pile to it.

Within five minutes he'd lost sight of her, which he hated, but from watching yesterday, he had a good idea what kind of distance any two searchers would keep from each other.

Not far.

Ten or fifteen minutes later, he caught a glimpse of the man Mara was trailing, whose white T-shirt stood out like a flag of surrender in these dim woods. Most of these men wore khaki cargo pants, some camouflage intended for dry country. Mara, he'd noted, had instinctively chosen blues and greens and browns that blended with the deep shadows. He knew she was close, but he didn't spot her.

*He* was on day three wearing the same shirt, because he hadn't thought through how best to blend in this wilderness when packing.

Damn it, where was Brianna?

HER THIRST GREW nearly unbearable, almost as bad as the pain from an arm so swollen, it looked fat. Bri realized she hadn't peed in a long time. Since yesterday or even the night before?

If she kept sitting here, she would die, and she didn't want to. She wanted to go *home*, even though she knew home didn't really exist anymore. With Mom dead… *Aunt Mara will take me*, Bri knew. She had faith, except right now Aunt Mara didn't know where Bri was, and how likely was she to stumble across this exact tree, even if she was somewhere in the vicinity searching?

The wells of these old trees made good hiding places, but this one was really deep. Could she get out, with only one arm to pull herself, only one hand she dared claw the earth and roots with? And what about her duffel? She *had* to take it, or she wouldn't have anything at all to eat or to wrap around herself again tonight.

*Throw the duffel*, she decided. If she stood up, it wasn't that far.

Even once she decided, she kept sitting there. Exhausted and hurting, she fell dull. Her head still ached, too. When she was like seven or eight, she didn't remember, she'd skidded on gravel when she was riding her bike and crashed into the curb. She'd broken her arm that time, too, and had what her mom called a goose egg on her head. She'd had to go to Emergency, where they'd cast her arm and then kept her overnight because of her head injury, what they called a concussion.

She wished like anything that she was lying in a hospital bed, where all she had to do was push a button to bring a nurse to find out what she wanted.

*I want* out *of here! I want to go home!*

More than that, she wanted all of this never to have happened. No other kid her age that she knew had had both parents die. Even if she got mad at Mom a lot, that was the worst part.

Slowly, painfully, she uncurled herself. She had to do this, but…just climbing to her feet was so hard. Ferns and other bushes that filled this big hole rustled with her movement and scratched at her arms and face. What if someone was close enough to hear? She stood absolutely still, waiting and listening.

Except she was swaying, without being able to help herself. Her head felt funny. She tried to lick her lips, but her tongue felt like she had a piece of beef jerky in her mouth instead. And her lips were dry, like the leaves that were fun to jump into after Aunt Mara raked them into a pile. When they lived in Bellingham, Mom paid some neighborhood kid to do it, so Bri would have been in big trouble if she'd ruined the piles. But she still remembered how they'd cushion her even as they crackled.

Cracked. That's what her lips had done. She quit trying to moisten them.

Now what?

Somehow, scramble up the dirt and moss wall in front of her that really wasn't any taller than she was, and it did have a slant instead of being straight up and down. She kept standing there for way too long.

Bri had forgotten the duffel and had to bend over to pick it up, making her head swim. Blinking hard, she straightened, half turned and swung with all her might. The duffel cleared the edge and tumbled out of sight.

Now her.

She grabbed what was probably a root with her good hand and pulled at the same time as she kicked the toes of her other foot into dirt. That lifted her a whole six inches. No, maybe more, but now she wanted to puke except she didn't have enough in her stomach and she couldn't stop now anyway.

There. She could grab that. It felt rough, with thorns that dug into her palm and fingers, but she used it to boost herself higher as her other foot sound some purchase. Then again. And again. And finally, she crawled over the lip of the hole she'd fallen so catastrophically into.

She lay there on her face, whimpering, until she heard…something. She found the strength to roll until she saw a man with a rifle pointed directly at her.

"Gotcha," he yelled.

She tried desperately to scramble away, but of course he grabbed her. By bad luck, his hand closed on her broken arm. Her vision blurred, and she screamed and screamed.

THE ONLY TIME Cam had ever heard screams like that was when he'd found a young soldier being tortured. He broke into the closest thing to a run he could manage on this steep sidehill and closed the distance rapidly. It helped that the creep who'd grabbed Brianna was whooping with pleasure almost as loud as her screams.

Mara was certain to hear. He spared a brief hope that she'd be in a position to take care of the man she had been shadowing before he could complicate the picture.

Ahead, Cam saw the stocky man wearing camouflage sling the slight girl over his shoulder. The screams became even more piercing, but Brianna also hammered his back with one fist and kicked at his stomach, thighs and everything in between.

That scum gave her a firm shake. "I'll dump you on your head if you don't stop that—"

She kept right on. Cam glimpsed her face, covered with tears and snot mixed with blood. Her mouth was open as she kept crying out. Struggling with her, the man didn't see Cam bounding toward him.

Cam approached from the back, swinging Bri to his own shoulder even as he punched the bastard midturn. She still sobbed. Cam didn't blame her. How would she know what was going on? But he felt her latch a hand onto his belt, which freed him to grab the rifle and slam a fist again into that loathsome creep's nose.

Blood spurted, and the guy staggered, yanking out his handgun. A perfectly planted knee, and he fell backward, but he managed to pull the trigger once before he landed in the tree well behind him. He didn't move again.

Ignoring a new burn in his arm, Cam swung around, tense, weapon in hand, searching for movement even as he cursed himself for giving the guy time to shoot.

THE BLOOD-CURDLING SCREAM had to be Bri. It had to be. Mara's heart rose even as she saw the fool in the white shirt spin and try to run, falling to his knees immediately. With that shirt, he might as well be wearing a target on his back. She wanted, with all the hate inside her, to shoot him, but a gunshot would draw a crowd. The very fact that he'd turned so that he didn't see her coming was an invitation to repeat her tactics with Davis.

The man didn't hear the small snick as she unsnapped her holster or her gasps for breath. His head jerked up as a gunshot split the silence.

*Not Cam. Not Bri. Please.*

Bri's screams lowered to wrenching sobs but loud enough to cover Mara's approach. She closed in, fingers clenched around the barrel of her gun, and swung.

He must have heard her at the last minute, because he started to turn. Too late. The butt of her gun connected just behind his temple with the same sickening thud as the last time she did this. He didn't go right down, though; he stumbled drunkenly and seemed to be fumbling for his own handgun or maybe the rifle over his shoulder.

She didn't give him a chance to clutch at either. She swung again, this time smashing into his nose. He was crumbling as she hit him yet again.

This time, he didn't move.

She dropped to her own knees, just to catch her breath. Or was it a sob?

Bri wasn't crying as hard because Mara heard a calm male voice saying, "I've got you, honey. You're safe now. I have you. Shh. Your aunt Mara is here, too. And you know me. I'm Deputy Frasier. Shh."

Mara dragged herself to her feet and stumbled and slid toward that voice and the sound of Brianna's crying. Hot tears ran down her own face.

*Alive! They're both alive! Thank you, God! Thank you.*

## *Chapter Sixteen*

The familiarity of that voice registered with Bri at last. This was the tall man Aunt Mara had dated. He was a police officer. It was still hard to quit crying, except her sobs were so dry they made her throat burn.

"Shh, shh," he kept murmuring, even as he rotated slowly, watching for something or someone.

Aunt Mara? Or any of the other men Bri had glimpsed over the past days? Oh no! If her screams hadn't brought a whole bunch of them running, the gunshot would. And…had this man, the police officer, been shot?

And then he said, "Mara," and eased Bri to her feet, turning her to face her aunt, whose cheeks were wet.

Aunt Mara lunged forward as if to engulf her in a giant hug, except she stopped herself at the last second, her gaze taking in Bri's hunched stance and the way she held her arm with the other one.

"Oh, sweetheart. You're hurt." She shook her head. "Of course you're hurt. But you're alive! I've been so scared."

The police officer had kept one hand on Bri's back and shoulder, and now he cupped Aunt Mara's head with the other. It was like everything Bri had wanted for days and days. Only…

"We can't stay here," he murmured. "We have to run."

Her aunt knelt in front of her. "Can you walk?"

"Yes, but…" Her words spilled over. "My arm's broken and my head hurts and everything else does, too, and I'm so thirsty." Thirsty came out like *thurty*. Her tongue was sticking, but she could see that both adults had understood her.

The deputy sheriff lowered his pack, rooted briefly in it and produced a water bottle. Her gaze fastened on it. That was the best thing Bri had ever seen— No, she corrected herself immediately. Second best, after Aunt Mara. And…maybe even third, after the very big, solid man with the soft voice who had stolen her back from that awful man as if there was nothing to it.

Now, he unscrewed the top, held the bottle for Bri and tipped it up slowly. The water was probably warm and tasted like the purifiers hikers always used, but it was still amazing. Her mouth soaked it up so that she didn't even have to swallow, except she then took another mouthful and another, until he pried the bottle out of her hand. "Enough for now. You don't want to make yourself sick."

"You're bleeding!" Aunt Mara exclaimed, looking over the top of Bri's head. "Did he shoot you?"

The police officer twisted to look at something. "Grazed me, maybe. Nothing to worry about."

He had. He'd been shot.

"Did you…did you see Mom?" Bri asked.

Aunt Mara's arm tightened around her. "I'm so sorry."

Now she had enough moisture to allow more tears. Only a few, but they stung.

"We have to go. *Now*," the police officer said with

new tension in his voice. "I know it hurts, but I'll have to carry you."

"I'll take your pack." Aunt Mara swung it onto her back even as she spoke.

"You lead the way," he said.

"Let's backtrack a little," she suggested.

He gently touched Bri's head, unerringly finding one of her lumps. "This is going to hurt, honey."

She managed to nod. "It's okay."

The way he smiled at her, she could totally see why her aunt liked him. And then he crouched, let her climb onto his back as best she could and straightened, arms looped under her knees. She grabbed on with her good arm, and knew this would hurt as much as it had when the bad guy found her.

But she *had* to stifle her cries. She had to.

THERE WAS NO such thing as a safe haven. Mara's goal was to guide them as far away from where that gun had been fired as she possibly could. She'd like to think men lingering by the wreckage on the creek wouldn't have heard the shot, but that was a gamble she, Cam and Bri couldn't afford.

Bri whimpered a few times, and Cam murmured to her, but Mara kept moving. *Run*, Cam had said, and that was what they were doing even on the plunging side of a river valley that didn't permit any speed but an awkward short step/long step.

But…they'd found Bri. She was safe—at least, as safe as they were. And they were armed. She suspected both the dirtbags she and Cam had started the morning by shadowing were dead. If not, they had to be in bad shape. They *deserved* to be, she told herself fiercely.

A shout drifted to her, followed by another. Neither were close by. She kept going until, at a touch on her shoulder, she stopped and turned.

Cam said, "I need to use the radio."

"But…those men must be spread over a mile every direction!"

"Yeah, but they'll gather again before dusk, and just in case they find the latest bodies and panic, I want the team close enough to descend on them before they can summon their own helicopter and make a getaway."

Bri looked dazed, and Mara wondered if she had any idea what they were talking about. It didn't matter, though; there was no hope of shielding her after everything she'd gone through this past week.

"Okay. Where's the radio?"

"Side pocket." He turned her, unzipped and took out the radio. She kissed Bri's cheek, pulled her Glock and moved to a slightly higher position that gave her a wider viewpoint. Bracing herself on a tree trunk, she made sure her stance was solid. All she wanted was to take Bri into her arms, but they didn't have time, not yet.

The sound of his strong voice and the crackle and responding voice made her wince, but she stayed on guard. The odds were against any of those men being near enough to hear. She didn't try to follow the conversation.

Realizing quiet had again fallen, except for Bri's ragged breathing, Mara looked at him.

"Let me stow this again."

He climbed to her instead of the other way around

and dropped his radio into the same pocket, then turned his head although he probably couldn't see Bri's face anyway.

"Hey, kiddo. You holding up there?"

"Kinda," she whispered.

"I want to set your arm and check your other injuries, but I think we'd better open some more distance first. We can get some pain meds in you before we go on, though."

"Really?" she whispered.

"Really."

Mara could tell he didn't want to stay where they were even that long, but he lowered himself to his knees and let Bri find her footing. Mara had circled behind him to dig in the pack and locate a first aid kit and a bottle of ibuprofen.

He agreed that was the strongest he had and let her decide what dose a girl who probably didn't weigh more than half what Mara did dared take. As he had earlier, she tipped the water bottle so Bri didn't have to do anything but swallow.

This first clear look at Bri's face made Mara sick. The bruises and blood and discoloration were nothing; what worried her most was the vague, even trancelike look in her eyes. They knew she'd suffered a head injury. How she had gone on this long, Mara couldn't imagine. And the arm…no, they didn't dare stop long enough to set a broken bone, and Mara suspected Bri wouldn't be able to help crying out as they handled it.

Pack zipped up again, Mara waited for Cam's nod before she went on. At a guess, they might be almost directly above the crash site. This was an area that would have been searched first, she had to believe.

Perhaps an hour later, she had a bad feeling if they dropped directly down toward the creek, she might come on Reggie Davis's body, assuming an animal hadn't dragged it away by now.

She glanced over her shoulder. Cam's gaze met hers.

"Watch for someplace we can hunker down."

Bri's condition had deteriorated even in this short time—or maybe with the pain slightly muffled, she was sagging toward sleep?

What if—? Mara gave herself a mental slap. Bri had been able to answer questions coherently. Focus, don't worry about brain damage.

Brighter sky showed ahead and above their elevation. She veered that way, almost cheering at the sight of a narrow talus slope that had plunged down a wrinkle in this up and down landscape. Boulders lay tipped against each other. This had to have happened in the past couple of years, or it would be more overgrown, but she spotted a mostly clear spot protected by a sort of rock-tepee.

A minute later, they lowered themselves to their knees and Mara was able to curve an arm around Bri. She wavered but still stood strong.

"I'm so proud of you," Mara told her softly. "Now let us take a look at your injuries."

Her niece blinked a few times, sniffed and said, "Okay."

Cam had hoped the break in Bri's upper arm was what was called a greenstick fracture, most common with kids, whose bones were more flexible than an adult's. But no. Once he'd used a knife to slice open the sleeves of a shirt and a fleece top, he saw at once that the extreme swelling complicated setting the bone. They had no ice, and he doubted ice would have diminished the swelling much anyway, given that the break had happened at least a day and probably two days ago. Bri seemed confused about it, and he understood.

Finally, he did his best with a foam, wrap-around splint that didn't equal a proper setting and casting but might offer enough support to ease the pain when she moved. Then he cut up another shirt to make a sling. He couldn't do anything for the bumps on the poor kid's head, either, which didn't sit well with him.

Mara insisted he bare his arm and let her clean what, from his perspective, wasn't much more than a gash. When she pulled out a package of gauze pads, he opened his mouth to tell her not to bother. She scowled at him. He held out the arm obediently and let her wrap it. It more than stung now, but he'd suffered a lot worse.

He'd be more worried about their current situation if he believed the three of them would have to seriously go on the run with no end in sight. As it was, once the tactical team had taken over the crash site and subdued everyone there, presumably it would be safe to make their way down and hitch a ride out of the national park.

His job now was to make sure the three of them remained unseen, and therefore safe, for the rest of the day.

Maybe he'd spent too much time beneath the high canopy of evergreens with the green light that almost felt like being underwater. He felt uneasy now, as if they were exposed even though he had initially liked the protection of the boulders.

Undecided, he made another call, this time to the county sheriff asking if he could spare the manpower to surround the resort and ensure that no one was able to flee until he and a team of other agents could search and separate the chaff from the wheat, so to speak; presumably, some of the construction personnel were just that. They agreed on a time.

Cam wished he didn't feel as if he was missing something.

Crouched beside Bri and Mara, he felt his heart give a hard squeeze at the sight of their battered faces and the trust in their eyes. He wasn't satisfied at how he'd done protecting either of them so far.

He checked to be sure his rifle was ready to fire, then held still and listened for a good minute, hearing only the reassuring activity of small mammals and birds.

Then he said, "Brianna, can you tell us what happened to cause the plane to crash?"

She started to cry again. At least, the hydrating was having an impact, although he had to wonder how far the sound of her sobs carried.

Her tale was muddled and incomplete, but he understood enough.

Dennis had stolen something, and Mom had known. Bri could tell, and even now she seemed shocked that her mother had been willing to go along with something like that. They'd left really early, in the dark, and Dennis hadn't turned on runway lights or any lights on the plane. He hadn't even done a precheck, which meant Bri had already been scared when another plane appeared not far behind them as the sky was lightening. Dennis had tried to shake it, but the worse part was when it came up beside them, and Bri saw a man with a rifle.

"I couldn't *hear* him shoot, but he did. There was a

bullet hole through the window glass really close to me." She swallowed. "And then he kept firing, and I knew Dennis had been shot. I couldn't tell if the plane just fell or if he tried to land it."

She'd been surprised to be alive, hurting but not severely injured. Cam steered her past locating her mother and Terrell, and then the hunt for the rear section of plane.

He stopped her before she launched into the saga of running and hiding.

"Do you know *what* Dennis stole?" he asked her.

She bit her lip, which made him wince as cracked as it was, then nodded. "He put this big duffel in the plane. Like, last thing. On the seat right beside me." She explained what it looked like and why she'd been curious and gotten into trouble for trying to open the zipper enough to peek into it.

By this time, she had hunched into a little ball within the circle of Mara's embrace, and Mara was glaring at him. Cam understood, but it pissed him off a little anyway. However, he also knew that *she* understood that they had to locate that duffel bag.

"After I saw Mom," Bri whispered, "I cried, and then I was mad, too. And scared."

For good reason.

Apparently, Dennis had yelled something about a tracker on the plane. Bri had found what she thought might be one and thrown it in the creek.

When Cam was that age, he'd have had no idea what a tracker was. Now he listened to what was an astonishing grasp of the ugly situation, of her hauling the bag—

"It was really heavy!"—into the woods and hiding it as best she could. And yes, she knew what was in it.

After hearing what she'd found, Cam grinned at her. "Now we know why they're so mad. You, Brianna Dawson, are so smart and brave, I'll recommend the Federal Bureau of Investigation hires you when you're old enough."

She giggled. It didn't last long, because it probably hurt. Mara laid her cheek atop her niece's head, and he wished he could wrap his arms around both of them and soak in the victory.

But he knew better than to celebrate prematurely.

They stayed where they were for the rest of the afternoon. Bri heard Cam—that's what he said to call him— tell Aunt Mara that this seemed as safe as anywhere. As comfortable, too.

They discussed whether it was worthwhile going back for their packs and decided not. They hadn't left anything they couldn't replace.

After a few hours, they gave Bri more ibuprofen, which didn't really help that much. But just sitting still, cuddled between Aunt Mara and Cam, Bri felt better than she had since Mom, yelling, had yanked her out of bed in what felt like the middle of the night.

Bri couldn't remember how many days ago that was. It seemed like forever. She didn't let herself think about the fact that the house her mom and Dennis had rented would never be home again, that they were both dead, and that when she went back to school, everyone would know and feel sorry for her.

She hunched a little when she thought that, wishing

she didn't *have* to go back to that school. She ordered herself not to think about that until later.

She kept sneaking looks at Cam, who looked dangerous even when he was relaxed. How did he do that? Maybe just his size and obvious strength, maybe the lines on his face, maybe the weapons he carried. It was kind of reassuring, except as the sun went down, he got more and more tense. At first he didn't even move, but she could feel his muscles tightening. Aunt Mara, too, she realized.

They were listening and waiting for a helicopter that was supposed to rescue them. Bri never again wanted to ride in a helicopter *or* an airplane, especially now that she knew what falling from the sky was really like, but she didn't say a word. If it would take her home, she could stand almost anything.

Once, Cam lifted his rifle, and Bri, too, saw a man slipping through the trees downhill from them. She held her breath, and Mara squeezed her hand. But the man never turned his head, and Cam let him pass.

A distant hum was the first any of them noticed. It got louder and louder, and the black dot she fixed her eyes on grew into a helicopter bigger than any she'd ever seen. Shadows from the mountains crept over them just as the helicopter stopped really close without setting down, and men wearing some kind of armor and carrying *big* rifles slid down ropes.

There was yelling and a few gunshots and more yelling. Cam's fingers flexed as if he wanted to be there. Aunt Mara and Cam were frozen, staring in that direction.

At last, Cam's radio crackled to life from where he'd

left it sitting on a rock, and he answered. Bri mostly heard what he said.

"How many? Anybody hurt?" And finally, "We'll make our way down to you. Don't shoot us."

Whoever he was talking to laughed. Bri didn't think what he'd said was at all funny. When he stowed the radio, he said, "Let's get going while there's still some light to see by." She wanted them to be safe now, for this to be all over, except the next thing he said was, "Since we don't have any count of how many men were dropped here to look for Bri and their money, we need to be careful. There might be a couple who managed to take off or just weren't back in time to be rounded up."

Aunt Mara rolled her eyes. "Really? How are we supposed to be *careful*?"

His one-sided smile was clearly just for her. In fact, he leaned over Bri and kissed her aunt. Only on the cheek, but still.

Then he helped Bri to her feet and knelt for her to climb onto his back again. Aunt Mara slung the pack on and grabbed the rifle, shaking her head when he reached for it.

"You need both your hands."

She was the first one to stand up. The moment she did, a gunshot rang out, and she dropped. As she fell, she flattened Bri and bumped into Cam.

Filled with horror, Bri wormed her way out from under Aunt Mara to find Cam had grabbed the rifle and crouched over them both, his expression enraged.

# Chapter Seventeen

Despite gut-deep terror, Cam zeroed in with his rifle on the two men who scrambled toward him firing wildly as they came. On the job, he had snipers on call, but he'd received sniper training in his second army deployment and learned the detachment to keep his hands steady until he saw the moment to pull the trigger.

Once. Red blossomed on the guy's chest, and he crashed backward. The second one tripped, rolled and leaped up to flee. Cam fought the desire to shoot to kill anyway. He breathed slowly, and in a matter of seconds regained the control to put a bullet in the attacker's thigh instead of his heart. With a scream, that guy fell, too, his rifle flying from his hands.

Cam didn't dare even look down at Mara. He was too afraid of what he'd see. Instead, he laid down the rifle and pulled his handgun, holding it in firing position as he approached the two. The one lay still, eyes open and glazed; the other writhed and tried for his holstered weapon when he saw Cam coming.

"Hands above your head!" he snapped. "That's it. You might live if you do what I say."

He prodded the dead man with his booted foot, just to be sure, then took enough steps to stand directly above the injured fellow. Bending over cautiously, he took the handgun from the holster and laid it a safe distance away. Damn, he wished he had cuffs, but Bri was in no condition to help, and Mara—

He couldn't think about her yet. He pushed back at the fear, astonished to see that his hands were completely steady.

His stomach clenched when he heard a crunch on rock right behind him. Surely not Bri—

But it was Mara who appeared in the corner of his eye, taking the rifle and pistol away from the dead man, setting them down and then joining him with her own handgun extended. "What do we do with him?"

"You're not hurt." *Now* his hands shook.

"A few new bruises. I'm sorry I fell on top of the two of you."

"I thought you'd been shot." He sounded like an automaton. "I couldn't—" He felt as if his throat had swelled shut.

"Couldn't what?" She gazed up at him in apparent perplexity.

"If I'd lost you now—" He was behaving like a petrified twenty-year-old, incoherent even as he said more than he should.

The man on the ground glared hatefully at them, his teeth clenched.

The thought that formed clear as a bell in Cam's head reawakened his terror. What if these weren't the only two who'd escaped the roundup? And here he stood, a perfect target and letting Mara be one, too, because he'd been too traumatized to use his damn head.

But before he could decide whether they should retreat to their rocks, a voice called from down below.

"Agent Frasier? That you?"

"It's me," he called back. "I need handcuffs."

"Always have some." Two men in full body armor emerged from the trees.

Beside Cam, Mara lowered her gun, then holstered it and turned to clamber back to Bri. Cam ignored his irrational feeling of abandonment, something that made no sense.

Once he got a better look at the two tac team members, he recognized both and greeted them by name.

"You didn't leave much for us to do," one of them remarked. "We only found five at their encampment."

"Two more here, two more—no, three more—I think Ms. Dawson and I brought down earlier. One of us will have to lead you to them." Maybe he could recover their packs after all.

He holstered his own gun, letting Agent Morrison cuff the injured man while his partner gathered the scattered weapons. Then Cam returned to the woman and girl waiting for him with all the hope and trust on their battered faces that he could have ever asked for.

THE SHINY SILVER duffel bag stayed with Cam while Mara and Bri were lifted onboard the helicopter to sit just behind the pilot during the first trip out. Positioned behind them, all the wounded—four of the bad guys—were guarded by several tactical team members. The decision had been made to fly directly to the hospital in Bellingham, unload and return for the rest of the team.

Mara and Bri were clutching each other as they were

lifted into the belly of the copter. Cam stood directly below them, the hand he'd steadied them with lifting as if he was trying to sustain his hold. He'd have given almost anything to go with them—but he had to do his job.

Mara surely understood that. She gave him one fraught look over her shoulder before she moved out of his sight, still holding her niece. He wished he could decipher that look.

As the helicopter rose and swooped into a long turn, a voice came from behind Cam.

"That's a heck of a kid." It was Paul Harris, who led this team.

Cam tore his gaze off the rapidly receding helicopter. "I'm still amazed she survived in the first place, never mind hid this damn thing–" he just refrained from kicking the duffel "—then got away from a full-out search for so long."

"Yeah." A solidly built man who had to be a few years older than Cam, Harris shook his head. "I could see them shooting down the guy who stole from them, but a woman and her child, too?" Yeah, that was disbelief, even though he'd undoubtedly seen as many ugly scenes, as much tragedy, as Cam had.

Cam would have given a lot to dig into that duffel and find out what was so important but couldn't, of course. They had to do this right, including having a crime scene investigator on hand. They might not find so much as a fingerprint except for Bri's on any of the bundles of money she had described, but they might, too. Anything that could bring down some important figures in this trafficking network would be worth more than whatever amount of money was contained in that bag. He gritted his teeth, assigned two tac team members to stay on guard, and led Paul and a couple of others with folding stretchers into the woods.

He didn't look forward to seeing the condition of the bodies he and Mara had strewn behind them. Any number of predators lived in this protected forest. Even at this time of year, the rain forest climate hastened decomposition.

On the other hand, he itched to dig into the computers and phones at the unfinished resort. As promised, Whatcom County deputies had rounded up everyone they found in the vicinity of the resort, but it had been late enough in the afternoon some workers had probably left. He had a suspicion most being held were bewildered construction workers. Dave Simmons was nowhere to be found, and neither were the two men who oversaw work in his absence. The six-seat airplane Cam had seen in the hangar was still there—or there again.

They did report a call Deputy Walker made after going to Dennis Terrell's rental home. Cam got directly in touch with him.

"Torn apart," Walker said. "Looks like it happened days ago. Even if it was in the middle of the night, I'm surprised no one heard or saw anything. They ripped up vinyl, dumped out all the food in the refrigerator, tossed it over. Some of it was a search, but a lot of the damage had to be from rage. Stinks from rotting food. We closed the house back up, although if you'd prefer I can bring our CSI out to looks for prints and take photos."

"Why don't you do that," Cam agreed, hoping it would save Mara from seeing even more that would devastate her. He knew in one way that she was tougher than that, but vulnerable, too, in that this had been all that was left of her family. She'd lost a lot. "I doubt they'll find anything of interest, but have 'em be careful."

He also requested a check of Dave Simmons's house, a rental but one of a handful of fancier log homes in a modest town.

Walker called back to report that it appeared untouched. He hadn't gone in, because he saw nothing that would give him an excuse. "Through the window I saw a few dishes in the kitchen sink, like a man might leave after a quick breakfast when he needed to hurry in to work."

Cam felt certain that Dave Simmons was dead unless he'd had an escape plan he implemented once he understood that he was responsible for the fact that a sleazy pilot under his employment had stolen something the big guns would consider unacceptable.

Dead seemed likelier.

Bri appeared at last to be in a deep, relaxing sleep, thanks to help from the doctor. It had been three or four in the morning before her tests and casting had been completed and she was free to sleep, but she woke up every half hour or so with a nightmare. Ditto with her naps today. Sometimes, she came awake screaming and fighting.

Mara knew that scream. She'd heard it when that creep had pounced on Bri, slung her over his shoulder despite her agonizing pain. She had a very bad feeling she'd be hearing that same scream multiple times a night for a long time to come.

Cam had called twice, once this morning and then

midday. He'd had news both times. First, he'd sounded astonishingly gentle when he told her that Diana's house had been trashed, that she would find very little to salvage in it. Early evening, he reported that Dave Simmons's body had been found in the woods between the resort and town, unfortunately by two boys who were pretend-hunting when their parents thought they were down the street at a friend's.

More kids traumatized.

She felt hollow. Partly tired, partly... She wasn't sure. Her life had taken a U-turn, and not for the first time. She wanted to believe she would be enough for a girl who had just lost her mom but suspected it wouldn't be easy. This would be more complicated for a girl Bri's age than if Diana had been killed in a car accident, say. As it was, Bri would have to come to terms with her mother's choices, especially the one that had resulted in the crash.

Bri was to stay at the hospital at least tonight, and potentially tomorrow night as well. Infection had set in when a jagged bone in her arm had torn open skin, and given the ensuing days, they worried about sepsis. The concussion had been severe enough, too, they preferred to keep an eye on her for longer.

Thanks to the nurses, Mara had had a desperately needed shower. Someone had seen to it that what she'd been wearing was clean, so she could change back into her own clothes. And, thank goodness, she'd grabbed her keys, her phone and a slim wallet with her driver's license and debit card before leaving her pack behind.

Bri had survived. She'd be okay.

Mara felt ragged, though. She'd snatched what sleep she could, but it wasn't enough. Two weeks of sleep wouldn't be enough, and she knew that lack of sleep wasn't really her problem. She'd struggled when her one national guard deployment was over. This was like that. She'd killed men. She'd been terrified for the one person she loved…except that at some point she became terrified for a second person. And now…

Oh, she assumed she'd see him again. He probably had to interview her and Bri in case he'd missed an important detail, although he could send a minion, she supposed.

It was possible she'd never see him again. That explained a big part of that hollow inside her. It felt like the steep side slope. If she fell, she'd keep rolling down, maybe forever. Hey, she could have daytime nightmares if she wanted!

Speaking of falling… Just her luck to fall for a guy whose life had intersected so briefly with hers. The sad thing was, she was just as scared of what would happen if he did want a relationship with her.

*Coward*, she scolded herself.

Hearing footsteps coming down the hall and pausing outside the room, Mara pulled herself together, pushed up from her slump over the bed and straightened her shoulders.

"Bri is sleeping like a baby," she whispered as she turned her head expecting to see the nurse on shift.

Oh, God. It was Cam. A clean Cam, wearing chinos, a black T-shirt and a black windbreaker that undoubtedly said FBI across the back. It was unnerving to see the man she'd first met, been powerfully drawn to, and yet instinctively mistrusted.

"I'm glad to hear that." He used the low, slightly rough voice that couldn't be heard from more than a few feet away. His eyes searched her face. "I was hoping I could persuade you to leave Bri for long enough to get a good night's sleep."

"I—" Torn, she glanced at a peacefully sleeping Bri and then back to Cam's rugged, tired face. "I don't suppose you've gotten much sleep, either."

"No. We could get a hotel room so you can be close or drive back to Thunder Creek. Up to you."

Would he stay with her either way? She gave a shaky smile. "I'll feel guilty if Bri wakes with a bad nightmare, but...yes. Please."

He smiled. "Let's make it a hotel so you can get back here quick if Bri really needs you."

Of course he'd understand.

He stepped up beside her and gazed down at Bri for a long time, creases deepening even more in a face that she realized looked a decade older than it had when she first met him. She'd been wrong in seeing an overlay of this Cam, the one she had to believe she knew so well, with the man working undercover.

"You kept believing in her," he murmured.

She had to swallow the lump in her throat. "I think most of the time I was pretending."

He lifted his gaze to meet hers, his eyes dark and intense. "I want someone to believe in me that way."

"Someone?" she whispered.

"You." He shook his head. "This isn't the place."

This felt like a replay of the last days, when hope and despair alternated. Did he really mean what she wanted him to?

Bobbing her head, she collected her change of clothes, keys and all, then led the way to the nurses' station. The one behind the counter suggested a nearby hotel where families of patients often stayed and told her not to worry. Yes, they'd call if a crisis arose, but the nurse couldn't imagine that happening. She gave Mara a white plastic bag with a drawstring to carry her meager possessions in.

Mara and Cam walked to the elevator, rode down and walked out into a warm night without saying another word. He led her to the Whatcom County Sheriff's Department vehicle he'd been driving when they first met. Just before he started the engine, he said, "By the way, I did grab your pack. There's probably nothing in it you need right now, but it's in back."

Her sleeping bag was almost new, and she'd be glad eventually for the clothes, but he was right: she couldn't think of anything in it she currently needed. He did grab his, although it obviously contained little.

The hotel wasn't five minutes away. As they walked into the lobby, he asked, "Should I get two rooms? One with two beds? Or just one?"

Scared or not, this was a chance she had to take. "One, please."

He gave her a single look, eyes heated, before he proceeded to check them in as if this was every day for them. Alone in the elevator, she said, "I'm not on birth control."

"I can take care of that."

Of course he could; he seemed like a man who was always prepared for anything, including a sexual interlude.

Except…she didn't think that was what this was. Maybe she was naive to feel something very close to certainty where he was concerned, but all she had to do was think back to some of the things he'd said. Including, at the end, a choked *if I'd lost you…*

The minute they were in the room, he locked and tossed his pack without looking to see where it landed. His words and expression were raw. "I want you."

Mara let the bag dangling from her hand fall. "I want you, too," she admitted. That sounded shy, but she had reason for nerves, given that she was hoping for so much.

He backed her into the short wall right before the room opened up, cupped her face and studied her with the burning gaze she'd caught glimpses of before. Then he kissed her.

There was nothing tentative about this. Mara grabbed on and kissed him back with all the passion and need in her. She felt his erection against her belly and tried to climb him even as her tongue tangled with his.

He wrenched his mouth away from hers long enough to pick her up so that she could wrap her legs around his waist, where that long, hard ridge felt best. Then he kept kissing her as she rubbed against him until he swore, carried her the dozen feet to the bed and fell with her onto it.

None of this was familiar to her. She'd never been so desperate she lost all self-consciousness. She didn't worry about how her body would appear to him as he stripped her; instead she worked to strip him, too. She didn't understand for a moment when he pulled back, growling something, until she understood that he had to slip off his belt and lay his holstered weapon and phone on the side table. His boots took a moment to remove, too. While he did all that, she drank in the sight of powerful muscles flexing in his back and a couple of scars she'd ask him about another time. His skin was hot and smooth with nothing soft beneath it. She splayed her hands on his back. *At last.*

He started to roll back to her, muttered, "Wallet," and extracted some packets before he unzipped and shed his pants.

Mara's stomach clenched at this frontal view. She wanted to look, but mostly she wanted—needed—him to come down on top of her, to push apart her legs, to fill her. Instead, he ripped open a packet and covered himself.

Once he had her in his arms again, he kissed her as if he couldn't get enough of her taste, exploring her with those big, callused hands until she was so beyond ready. And even then, he paused to rub his cheek against her breast and suck once, hard. When her hips rose and she clutched at him, Cam lifted one of her thighs, the rest of his weight on an elbow, and pushed inside her.

It had been long enough, she'd half expected a moment of discomfort, but instead she felt gloriously full, this being exactly what she needed. When he pulled back, she cried a protest and grabbed him to bring him back.

She saw those molten gray eyes as he said her name from between bared teeth and let herself fly. She was all feeling, her brain not willing to second-guess yet. With a final hard thrust, Cam joined her, holding hard inside her, every muscle that she felt beneath her hands or could see rigid.

And still, when he relaxed, he came down on his shoulder and gathered her into his arms instantly. Careful; he was always careful with her.

It had to be a couple of minutes before anything she could call a thought intruded. Just as her brain considered forming a few words, he said in a voice she'd never heard before, "I want you in my bed every night."

Mara worked her mouth before she could answer, but when she did, she laid herself bare. "I do, too, but…it's not that simple."

"No." He tipped his head as if to try to see her face. "I know that. You're a mother. You have a job. We *both* have jobs. Mine…can be difficult for a partner."

They were back to trust. She threw a leg over him and pressed herself as close as was humanly possible in unspoken response for his old hurt, even as she knew only time would trúly reassure him.

His mouth grazed her forehead and his arms tightened, too.

"Do you have to leave tomorrow?" she asked after a moment.

"Day after, I think. I assume you'll want to stay with Bri tomorrow?"

"Mm."

"We can keep this room."

"Okay."

"Is it too soon to talk about how we can make this work?" A smile entered his voice. "I need a minute before I'm ready to go again anyway."

She felt her first flutter of panic. "I can't walk out on the school district." Would he see that as an excuse? But hiring a replacement willing to work in such a remote location was a challenge, especially in the middle of the school year. She'd been the only applicant when she had been hired. She couldn't treat the school district or her students that way. Although she was worried about something else altogether. "I need to find out whether Bri can stand to go back to school at Thunder Creek. Seeing her old house. You know." She swallowed. "We can…try to coordinate days off."

The pause was long enough to scare her. When he spoke, his tone was neutral. "That won't be easy."

Maybe it was just as well, considering how fast this had happened. "I do need time," she admitted. Trying to lighten the moment, she added, "Just don't tell me how many children we should have."

He chuckled. Feeling the rumble beneath her cheek was amazing. "That *would* be premature." From his smirk, she knew the choice of words had been deliberate.

Her laugh was something new. It was as if she were freeing herself, acknowledging the faith she'd lost in her own judgment but grateful she could be here, with this man.

Cam rolled away and went into the bathroom, presumably to dispose of the condom although she wondered if he thought she was letting him down easy instead of just being afraid to believe.

As he walked back to the bed, he said, "There'll be… stretches, like this one, where I'll be away."

She hadn't needed his second mention to tell her how sore this issue was for him. When he sat down, Mara wriggled over to plant a big kiss on his chest. With heartfelt sincerity, she told him, "I will never forget that you saved Bri's life during one of your absences. Every investigation is important, or you wouldn't be sent out."

The strangled sound from him was wordless but made her eyes sting. He surprised her then by asking, "No chance you'll get called back to the National Guard?"

She hadn't thought about that possibility in forever.

"I'm inactive. And now that I'm all Bri has for a parent… I can't imagine."

"I say we need to take advantage of tonight." He pushed himself up, gave a wicked grin, and kissed her. Lifting his head, he said, "If we can only manage to see each other every few weeks, then that's how it'll be until you're ready for more."

# *Epilogue*

Thank heavens the school year was starting to wind down. Mara crossed her fingers in hopes Cam could get away from work for at least a few days during what was the school's spring break. This was Friday, and Bri was just about to hop out of the car at her friend Hailey's house. Tonight, four girls were planning to celebrate. They'd spent ages on the phone the past few days—*teenage years, here we come*—deciding what they'd stream, what they especially wanted to eat, whether Hailey's mom would let them bake cookies. Maybe even two kinds.

Bri's hesitation surprised Mara. "Um…are you seeing Cam?"

"I'd like to think so, but I'm not sure. Why?"

Bri eyed her narrowly. "You *are* going to marry him, right?"

Mara laughed, hugged her and said, "Are you kidding? I'm not letting him get away."

"Cool."

And that was it. He was Bri's hero, after all. She grabbed her overnight bag and trotted up to the front door without a single glance back.

Unfortunately, Mara hadn't gotten any response to her text letting Cam know she'd be alone tonight.

So the last thing she expected was to see his SUV parked at the curb in front of her house. She pulled into the driveway and barely remembered to turn off the engine before she raced to meet him mid-lawn and throw herself into his arms.

As hard as it was to be separated most of the time, she still believed she'd made the right decision. A temporary change wouldn't have been good for Bri, and Mara didn't want to echo Diana's choice to move in right away with any new guy.

"I missed you," he said hoarsely, his cheek against the top of her head.

"I've missed you so much," she whispered, holding on tight.

The first few weeks hadn't been as bad, since his focus was wrapping up the mess Mara and Bri had inadvertently become involved in. There was a staggering amount of money in that duffel, but considering the cost of paying all the men sent to retrieve it, the cost/benefit basis was off, Cam had declared. It came as no surprise that, in fact, techs had come up with several fingerprints in the bag, including one on the note. That belonged to a major drug trafficker Canadian authorities had been circling around for a couple of years, and the fingerprint alone gave them the excuse they needed to close in on him. Better yet, a careless email linked the resort project with the already operating one close to the Mexican border. It gave federal agents investigating that one a wedge in.

And then, of course, he had worked with a detective

from Whatcom County investigating Dave Simmons's murder, still unsolved although they knew damn well who had ordered it.

Bri had begged not to have to go back to school in Thunder Creek at first, but since Mara was pretty well stuck in her job until school let out for the summer, it was fortunate that Bri's fame wore off fast. Kids her age forgot quickly that her mom had just died, never mind the rest of it.

The bad news for the community was that construction on the Thunder Creek resort was suspended. Victor Levin, the big money behind the resort, was still free, but undoubtedly trying to behave like an innocent man who was deeply shocked by how his project had been used. His attempt to find a purchaser for the half-built resort failed. The bones of the resort weren't literally in sight from downtown, but loomed nonetheless like a haunted mansion that scared everyone.

Mara led Cam inside now, telling him about the great party. He looked tired again, unsurprisingly, but laughed anyway. He and Bri hadn't given any hint that they weren't tight.

As he dropped his bag on the sofa, he said, "One piece of good news. I hear that a resort chain just closed on a deal for this one, probably for a song. They believe they can finish it and have it open by July."

"That's fantastic! This place could use the jobs. About a third of the kids in my class had to move away. I've gotten fond of Thunder Creek."

"Not too fond, I hope."

"You know better than that."

"Good." He seemed to hesitate, then plucked something from inside his leather bag. "Maybe I should wait, but…" He took a couple of steps to stand right in front of her, then said simply, "I love you, Mara. Will you marry me?" He flipped open a small jewelry box to let her see a gorgeous jade and diamond ring. "We can return this if you want something else, but since we spent most of our time up here in a green wonderland, I thought the color was appropriate."

"Oh, Cam." Her eyes stung, but she blinked away any incipient tears. "I love you, too. Of course I'll marry you!"

He slid the ring onto her finger, then tipped up her chin and gave her a devastatingly tender kiss. Looking down at her again, he asked, "Bri going to be okay with this?"

Mara was astonished she *could* laugh, given how crowded with emotion she felt. But when she told him about Bri's parting words, he chuckled. "She's like a mini Mara."

Blast it, now she *was* crying. He held her and rocked her slightly as he had in that first, horrible week. "Did I say something wrong?"

"No!" she all but wailed. "It's just…she does look more like me than she did like her mom, and maybe that was part of what Diana struggled with."

"It's not just looks, either."

"I don't know. Diana was no coward."

"No," he said gently. "Although I'm betting Bri has more common sense than her mom did."

Mara swiped away any remnant of tears on his shirt. "I can only hope." She hesitated. "She still has nightmares, but just the other day she told me she'd wished for a long time that she could live with me. Even if that wasn't totally true, we both ended up sobbing."

He brushed a few damp tendrils of escaped hair back from her forehead. "Somehow I'm not surprised, but… I'm glad."

If she sometimes felt guilty, she would never let Bri know that.

His gray eyes were softer than she ever remembered seeing them as he led her to the sofa and she snuggled up to him.

"Do we have to wait until summer to get married?"

"Any time is good for me." She offered him a tremulous smile. "You know, we won't see each other more often just because we're wearing wedding rings."

"True." He grimaced. "Even so, I'd be happier. I've started browsing real estate listings online. Saw one place I really like. I'll show it to you later."

"Oh, you mean after dinner?" she said with wide-eyed innocence, then was startled into a giggle when he lifted her onto his lap.

"Who needs dinner?" he said, before his mouth claimed hers.

* * * * *

# Get up to 4 Free Books!

## We'll send you 2 free books from each series you try
## PLUS a free Mystery Gift.

Both the **Harlequin Intrigue®** and **Harlequin® Romantic Suspense** series feature compelling novels filled with heart-racing action-packed romance that will keep you on the edge of your seat

**YES!** Please send me 2 FREE novels from the Harlequin Intrigue or Harlequin Romantic Suspense series and my FREE gift (gift is worth about $10 retail). I may cancel anytime by emailing ReaderServiceInfo@Harlequin.com or by calling 1-800-873-8635.If I don't cancel, I will receive 6 brand-new Harlequin Intrigue Larger-Print books every month and be billed just $7.19 each in the U.S. or $7.99 each in Canada, or 4 brand-new Harlequin Romantic Suspense books every month and be billed just $6.39 each in the U.S. or $7.19 each in Canada, a savings of 20% off the cover price. It's quite a bargain! Shipping and handling is just 75¢ per book in the U.S. and $1.75 per book in Canada.* I understand that accepting the free books and gift places me under no obligation to buy anything—they are mine to keep for free no matter what I decide.

Choose one:

☐ **Harlequin Intrigue Larger-Print** (199/399 BPA G3CD)

☐ **Harlequin Romantic Suspense** (240/340 BPA G3CD)

☐ **Or Try Both!** (199/399 & 240/340 BPA G3CE)

Name (please print)

Address    Apt. #

City    State/Province    Zip/Postal Code

**Email:** Please check this box ☐ if you would like to receive newsletters and promotional emails from Harlequin Enterprises ULC and its affiliates. You can unsubscribe anytime.

### Mail to the **Harlequin Reader Service:**
**IN U.S.A.:** P.O. Box 1341, Buffalo, NY 14240-8531
**IN CANADA:** P.O. Box 603, Fort Erie, Ontario L2A 5X3

Want to explore our other series or interested in ebooks? Visit **www.ReaderService.com** or call **1-800-873-8635.**